I0665433

TWO WORLDS OF EDMOND HAMILTON

THE STARS, MY BROTHERS

THE MONSTERS OF JUNTONHEIM

TWO WORLDS OF EDMOND HAMILTON

THE STARS, MY BROTHERS

THE MONSTERS OF JUNTONHEIM

WILDSIDE PRESS

TWO WORLDS OF EDMOND HAMILTON

"The Stars, My Brothers" originally appeared in
Amazing Stories Fact and Science Fiction May 1962.
"The Monsters of Juntonheim" originally appeared
in *Startling Stories,* January 1941.

CONTENTS

THE STARS,
MY BROTHERS

1.

SOMETHING TINY went wrong, but no one ever knew whether it was in an electric relay or in the brain of the pilot.

The pilot was Lieutenant Charles Wandek, UNRC, home address: 1677 Anstey Avenue, Detroit. He did not survive the crash of his ferry into Wheel Five. Neither did his three passengers, a young French astrophysicist, an East Indian expert on magnetic fields, and a forty-year-old man from Philadelphia who was coming out to replace a pump technician.

Someone else who did not survive was Reed Kieran, the only man in Wheel Five itself to lose his life. Kieran, who was thirty-six years old, was an accredited scientist-employee of UNRC. Home address: 815 Elm Street, Midland Springs, Ohio.

Kieran, despite the fact that he was a confirmed bachelor, was in Wheel Five because of a woman. But the woman who had sent him there was no beautiful lost love. Her name was Gertrude Lemmiken; she was nineteen years old and overweight, with a fat, stupid face. She suffered from head-colds, and sniffed constantly in the Ohio college classroom where Kieran taught Physics Two.

One March morning, Kieran could bear it no longer. He told himself, "If she sniffs this morning, I'm through. I'll resign and join the UNRC."

Gertrude sniffed. Six months later, having finished his training for the United Nations Reconnaissance Corps, Kieran shipped out for a term of duty in UNRC Space Laboratory Number 5, known more familiarly as Wheel Five.

Wheel Five circled the Moon. There was an elaborate base on the surface of the Moon in this year 1981. There were laboratories and observatories there, too. But it had been found that the alternating fortnights of boiling heat and near-absolute-zero cold on the lunar surface could play havoc with the delicate instruments used in certain researches. Hence Wheel Five had been built and was staffed by research men who were rotated at regular eight-month intervals.

*****

Kieran loved it, from the first. He thought that that was because of the sheer beauty of it, the gaunt, silver deaths-head of the Moon forever turning beneath, the still and solemn glory of the un-dimmed stars, the filamentaries stretched across the distant star-clusters like shining veils, the quietness, the peace.

But Kieran had a certain intellectual honesty, and after a while he admitted to himself that neither the beauty nor the romance of it was what made this life so attractive to him. It was the fact that he was far away from Earth. He did not even have to look at Earth, for nearly all geophysical research was taken care of by Wheels Two and Three that circled the mother planet. He was almost completely divorced from all Earth's problems and people.

Kieran liked people, but had never felt that he understood them. What seemed important to them, all the drives of ordinary day-to-day existence, had never seemed very important to him. He had felt that there must be something wrong with him, something lacking, for it seemed to him that people everywhere committed the most outlandish follies, believed in the most incredible things, were swayed by pure herd-instinct into the most harmful courses of behavior. They could not all be wrong, he thought, so he must be wrong — and it had worried him. He had taken partial refuge in pure science, but the study and then the teaching of astrophysics had not been the refuge that Wheel Five was. He would be sorry to leave the Wheel when his time was up.

And he was sorry, when the day came. The others of the staff were already out in the docking lock in the rim, waiting to greet the replacements from the ferry. Kieran, hating to leave, lagged behind. Then, realizing it would be churlish not to meet this young Frenchman who was replacing him, he hurried along the corridor in the big spoke when he saw the ferry coming in.

He was two-thirds of the way along the spoke to the rim when it happened. There was a tremendous crash that flung him violently from his feet. He felt a coldness, instant and terrible.

He was dying.

He was dead.

The ferry had been coming in on a perfectly normal approach when the tiny something went wrong, in the ship or in the judgment of the pilot. Its drive-rockets suddenly blasted on full, it heeled over sharply, it smashed through the big starboard spoke like a knife through butter.

Wheel Five staggered, rocked, and floundered. The automatic safety bulkheads had all closed, and the big spoke — Section T2 — was the only section to blow its air, and Kieran was the only man caught in it. The alarms went off, and while the wreckage of the ferry, with three dead men in it, was still drifting close by, everyone in the Wheel was in his pressure-suit and emergency measures were in full force.

*****

Within thirty minutes it became evident that the Wheel was going to survive this accident. It was edging slowly out of orbit from the impetus of the blow, and in the present weakened state of the construction its small corrective rockets could not be used to stop the drift. But Meloni, the UNRC captain commanding, had got first reports from his damage-control teams, and it did not look too bad. He fired off peremptory demands for the repair materials he would need, and was assured by UNRC headquarters at Mexico City that the ferries would be loaded and on their way as soon as possible.

Meloni was just beginning to relax a little when a young officer brought up a minor but vexing problem. Lieutenant Vinson had headed the small party sent out to recover the bodies of the four dead men. In their pressure-suits they had been pawing through the tangled wreckage for some time, and young Vinson was tired when he made his report.

"We have all four alongside, sir. The three men in the ferry were pretty badly mangled in the crash. Kieran wasn't physically wounded, but died from space-asphyxiation."

The captain stared at him. "Alongside? Why didn't you bring them in? They'll go back in one of the ferries to Earth for burial."

"But —" Vinson started to protest.

Meloni interrupted sharply. "You need to learn a few things about morale, Lieutenant. You think it's going to do morale here any good to have four dead men floating alongside where everyone can see them? Fetch them in and store them in one of the holds."

Vinson, sweating and unhappy now, had visions of a black mark on his record, and determined to make his point.

"But about Kieran, sir — he was only frozen. Suppose there was a chance to bring him back?"

"Bring him back? What the devil are you talking about?"

Vinson said, "I read they're trying to find some way of restoring a man that gets space-frozen. Some scientists down at Delhi University. If they succeeded, and if we had Kieran still intact in space —"

"Oh, hell, that's just a scientific pipe-dream, they'll never find a way to do that," Meloni said. "It's all just theory."

"Yes, sir," said Vinson, hanging his head.

"We've got trouble enough here without you bringing up ideas like this," the captain continued angrily. "Get out of here."

Vinson was now completely crushed. "Yes, sir. I'll bring the bodies in."

He went out. Meloni stared at the door, and began to think. A commanding officer had to be careful, or he could get skinned alive. If, by some remote chance, this Delhi idea ever succeeded, he, Meloni, would be in for it for having Kieran buried. He strode to the door and flung it open, mentally cursing the young snotty who had had to bring this up.

"Vinson!" he shouted.

The lieutenant turned back, startled. "Yes, sir?"

"Hold Kieran's body outside. I'll check on this with Mexico City."

"Yes, sir."

Still angry, Meloni shot a message to Personnel at Mexico City. That done, he forgot about it. The buck had been passed, let the boys sitting on their backsides down on Earth handle it.

Colonel Hausman, second in command of Personnel Division of UNRC, was the man to whom Meloni's message went. He snorted loudly when he read it. And later, when he went in to report to Garces, the brigadier commanding the Division, he took the message with him.

"Meloni must be pretty badly rattled by the crash," he said. "Look at this."

Garces read the message, then looked up. "Anything to this? The Delhi experiments, I mean?"

Hausman had taken care to brief himself on that point and was able to answer emphatically.

"Damned little. Those chaps in Delhi have been playing around freezing insects and thawing them out, and they think the process might be developed someday to where it could revive frozen space-men. It's an iffy idea. I'll burn Meloni's backside off for bringing it up at a time like this."

Garces, after a moment, shook his head. "No, wait. Let me think about this."

He looked speculatively out of the window for a few moments. Then he said,

"Message Meloni that this one chap's body — what's his name, Kieran? — is to be preserved in space against a chance of future revival."

Hausman nearly blotted his copybook by exclaiming, "For God's sake —" He choked that down in time and said, "But it could be centuries before a revival process is perfected, if it ever is."

Garces nodded. "I know. But you're missing a psychological point that could be valuable to UNRC. This Kieran has relatives, doesn't he?"

Hausman nodded. "A widowed mother and a sister. His father's been dead a long time. No wife or children."

Garces said, "If we tell them he's dead, frozen in space and then buried, it's all over with. Won't those people feel a lot better if we tell them that he's *apparently* dead, but might be brought back when a revival-technique is perfected in the future?"

"I suppose they'd feel better about it," Hausman conceded. "But I don't see —"

Garces shrugged. "Simple. We're only really beginning in space, you know. As we go on, UNRC is going to lose a number of men, space-struck just like Kieran. A howl will go up about our casualty lists, it always does. But if we can say that they're only frozen until such time as revival technique is achieved, everyone will feel better about it."

"I suppose public relations are important —" Hausman began to say, and Garces nodded quickly.

"They are. See that this is done, when you go up to confer with Meloni. Make sure that it gets onto the video networks, I want everyone to see it."

Later, with many cameras and millions of people watching, Kieran's body, in a pressure-suit, was ceremoniously taken to a selected position where it would orbit the Moon. All suggestions of the funerary were carefully avoided. The space-struck man — nobody at all referred to him as "dead" — would remain in this position until a revival process was perfected.

"Until forever," thought Hausman, watching sourly. "I suppose Garces is right. But they'll have a whole graveyard here, as time goes on."

As time went on, they did.

2.

IN HIS dreams, a soft voice whispered.

He did not know what it was telling him, except that it was important. He was hardly aware of its coming, the times it came. There would be the quiet murmuring, and something in him seemed to hear and understand, and then the murmur faded away and there was nothing but the dreams again.

But were they dreams? Nothing had form or meaning. Light, darkness, sound, pain and not-pain, flowed over him. Flowed over — who? Who was he? He did not even know that. He did not care.

But he came to care, the question vaguely nagged him. He should try to remember. There was more than dreams and the whispering voice. There was — what? If he had one real thing to cling to, to put his feet on and climb back from — One thing like his name.

He had no name. He was no one. Sleep and forget it. Sleep and dream and listen —

"Kieran."

It went across his brain like a shattering bolt of lightning, that word. He did not know what the word was or what it meant but it found an echo somewhere and his brain screamed it.

"Kieran!"

Not his brain alone, his voice was gasping it, harshly and croakingly, his lungs seeming on fire as they expelled the word.

He was shaking. He had a body that could shake, that could feel pain, that was feeling pain now. He tried to move, to break the nightmare, to get back again to the vague dreams, and the soothing whisper.

He moved. His limbs thrashed leadenly, his chest heaved and panted, his eyes opened.

He lay in a narrow bunk in a very small metal room.

He looked slowly around. He did not know this place. The gleaming white metal of walls and ceiling was unfamiliar. There was a slight, persistent tingling vibration in everything that was unfamiliar, too.

He was not in Wheel Five. He had seen every cell in it and none of them were like this. Also, there lacked the persistent susurrant sound of the ventilation pumps. Where —

You're in a ship, Kieran. A starship.

Something back in his mind told him that. But of course it was ridiculous, a quirk of the imagination. There weren't any starships.

You're all right, Kieran. You're in a starship, and you're all right.

The emphatic assurance came from somewhere back in his brain and it was comforting. He didn't feel very good, he felt dopey and sore, but there was no use worrying about it when he knew for sure he was all right —

The hell he was all right! He was in someplace new, someplace strange, and he felt half sick and he was not all right at all. Instead of lying here on his back listening to comforting lies from his imagination, he should get up, find out what was going on, what had happened.

Of a sudden, memory began to clear. What *had* happened? Something, a crash, a terrible coldness —

Kieran began to shiver. He had been in Section T2, on his way to the lock, and suddenly the floor had risen under him and Wheel Five had seemed to crash into pieces around him. The cold, the pain —

You're in a starship. You're all right.

For God's sake why did his mind keep telling him things like that, things he believed? For if he did not believe them he would be in a panic, not knowing where he was, how he had come here. There was panic in his mind but there was a barrier against it, the barrier of the soothing reassurances that came from he knew not where.

He tried to sit up. It was useless, he was too weak. He lay, breathing heavily. He felt that he should be hysterical with fear but somehow he was not, that barrier in his mind prevented it.

He had decided to try shouting when a door in the side of the little room slid open and a man came in.

He came over and looked down at Kieran. He was a young man, sandy-haired, with a compact, chunky figure and a flat, hard face. His eyes were blue and intense, and they gave Kieran the feeling that this man was a wound-up spring. He looked down and said,

"How do you feel, Kieran?"

Kieran looked up at him. He asked, "Am I in a starship?"

"Yes."

"But there aren't any starships."

"There are. You're in one." The sandy-haired man added, "My name is Vaillant."

It's true, what he says, murmured the something in Kieran's mind.

"Where — how —" Kieran began.

Vaillant interrupted his stammering question. "As to where, we're quite a way from Earth, heading right now in the general direction of Altair. As to how —" He paused, looking keenly down at Kieran. "Don't you know how?"

Of course I know. I was frozen, and now I have been awakened and time has gone by —

Vaillant, looking searchingly down at his face, showed a trace of relief. "You do know, don't you? For a moment I was afraid it hadn't worked."

He sat down on the edge of the bunk.

"How long?" asked Kieran.

Vaillant answered as casually as though it was the most ordinary question in the world. "A bit over a century."

It was wonderful, thought Kieran, how he could take a statement like that without getting excited. It was almost as though he'd known it all the time.

"How —" he began, when there was an interruption.

Something buzzed thinly in the pocket of Vaillant's shirt. He took out a thin three-inch disk of metal and said sharply into it, "Yes?"

A tiny voice squawked from the disk. It was too far from Kieran for him to understand what it was saying but it had a note of excitement, almost of panic, in it.

Something changed, hardened, in Vaillant's flat face. He said, "I expected it. I'll be right there. You know what to do."

He did something to the disk and spoke into it again. "Paula, take over here."

He stood up. Kieran looked up at him, feeling numb and stupid. "I'd like to know some things."

"Later," said Vaillant. "We've got troubles. Stay where you are."

He went rapidly out of the room. Kieran looked after him, wondering. Troubles — troubles in a starship? And a century had passed —

He suddenly felt an emotion that shook his nerves and tightened his guts. It was beginning to hit him now. He sat up in the bunk and swung his legs out of it and tried to stand but could not, he was too weak. All he could do was to sit there, shaking.

His mind could not take it in. It seemed only minutes ago that he had been walking along the corridor in Wheel Five. It seemed that Wheel Five must exist, that the Earth, the people, the time he knew, must still be somewhere out there. This could be some kind of a joke, or some kind of psychological experiment. That was it — the space-medicine boys were always making way-out experiments to find out how men would bear up in unusual conditions, and this must be one of them —

A woman came into the room. She was a dark woman who might have been thirty years old, and who wore a white shirt and slacks. She would, he thought, have been good-looking if she had not looked so tired and so edgy.

She came over and looked down at him and said to him,

"Don't try to get up yet. You'll feel better very soon."

Her voice was a slightly husky one. It was utterly familiar to Kieran, and yet he had never seen this woman before. Then it came to him.

"You were the one who talked to me," he said, looking up at her. "In the dreams, I mean."

She nodded. "I'm Paula Ray and I'm a psychologist. You had to be psychologically prepared for your awakening."

"Prepared?"

The woman explained patiently. "Hypnopedic technique — establishing facts in the subconscious of a sleeping patient. Otherwise, it would be too terrific a shock for you when you awakened. That was proved when they first tried reviving space-struck men, forty or fifty years ago."

The comfortable conviction that this was all a fake, an experiment of some kind, began to drain out of Kieran. But if it was true —

He asked, with some difficulty, "You say that they found out how to revive space-frozen men, that long ago?"

"Yes."

"Yet it took forty or fifty years to get around to reviving me?"

The woman sighed. "You have a misconception. The process of revival was perfected that long ago. But it has been used only immediately after a wreck or disaster. Men or women in the old space-cemeteries have not been revived."

"Why not?" he asked carefully.

"Unsatisfactory results," she said. "They could not adjust psychologically to changed conditions. They usually became unbalanced. Some suicides and a number of cases of extreme schizophrenia resulted. It was decided that it was no kindness to the older space-struck cases to bring them back."

"But you brought me back?"

"Yes."

"Why?"

"There were good reasons." She was, clearly, evading that question. She went on quickly. "The psychological shock of awakening would have been devastating, if you were not prepared. So, while you were still under sedation, I used the hypnopedic method on you. Your unconscious was aware of the main facts of the situation before you awoke, and that cushioned the shock."

Kieran thought of himself, lying frozen and dead in a graveyard that was space, bodies drifting in orbit, circling slowly around each other as the years passed, in a macabre sarabande — A deep shiver shook him.

"Because all space-struck victims were in pressure-suits, dehydration was not the problem it could have been," Paula was saying. "But it's still a highly delicate process —"

He looked at her and interrupted roughly. "What reasons?" And when she stared blankly, he added, "You said there were good reasons why you picked me for revival. What reasons?"

Her face became tight and alert. "You were the oldest victim, in point of date. That was one of the determining factors —"

"Look," said Kieran. "I'm not a child, nor yet a savage. You can drop the patronizing professional jargon and answer my question."

Her voice became hard and brittle. "You're new to this environment. You wouldn't understand if I told you."

"Try me."

"All right," she answered. "We need you, as a symbol, in a political struggle we're waging against the Sakae."

"The Sakae?"

"I told you that you couldn't understand yet," she answered impatiently, turning away. "You can't expect me to fill you in on a whole world that's new to you, in five minutes."

She started toward the door. "Oh, no," said Kieran. "You're not going yet."

He slid out of the bunk. He felt weak and shaky but resentment energized his flaccid muscles. He took a step toward her.

The lights suddenly went dim, and a bull-throated roar sounded from somewhere, an appalling sound of raw power. The slight tingling that Kieran had felt in the metal fabric around him abruptly became a vibration so deep and powerful that it dizzied him and he had to grab the stanchion of the bunk to keep from falling.

Alarm had flashed into the woman's face. Next moment, from some hidden speaker in the wall, a male voice yelled sharply,

"Overtaken — prepare for extreme evasion —"

"Get back into the bunk," she told Kieran.

"What is it?"

"It may be," she said with a certain faint viciousness, "that you're about to die a second time."

3.

THE LIGHTS dimmed to semi-darkness, and the deep vibration grew worse. Kieran clutched the woman's arm.

"What's happening?"

"Damn it, let me go!" she said.

The exclamation was so wholly familiar in its human angriness that Kieran almost liked her, for the first time. But he continued to hold onto her, although he did not feel that with his present weakness he could hold her long.

"I've a right to know," he said.

"All right, perhaps you have," said Paula. "We — our group — are operating against authority. We've broken laws, in going to Earth and reviving you. And now authority is catching up to us."

"Another ship? Is there going to be a fight?"

"A fight?" She stared at him, and shock and then faint repulsion showed in her face. "But of course, you come from the old time of wars, you would think that —"

Kieran got the impression that what he had said had made her look at him with the same feelings he would have had when he looked at a decent, worthy savage who happened to be a cannibal.

"I always felt that bringing you back was a mistake," she said, with a sharpness in her voice. "Let me go."

She wrenched away from him and before he could stop her she had got to the door and slid it open. He woke up in time to lurch after her and he got his shoulder into the door-opening before she could slide it shut.

"Oh, very well, since you insist I'm not going to worry about you," she said rapidly, and turned and hurried away.

Kieran wanted to follow her but his knees were buckling under him. He hung to the side of the door-opening. He felt angry, and anger was all that kept him from falling over. He would not faint, he told himself. He was not a child, and would not be treated like one —

He got his head outside the door. There was a long and very narrow corridor out there, blank metal with a few closed doors along it. One door, away down toward the end of the corridor, was just sliding shut.

He started down the corridor, steadying himself with his hand against the smooth wall. Before he had gone more than a few steps, the anger that pushed him began to ebb away. Of a sudden, the mountainous and incredible fact of his being here, in this place, this time, this ship, came down on him like an avalanche from which the hypnopedic pre-conditioning would no longer protect him.

I am touching a starship, I am in a starship, I, Reed Kieran of Midland Springs, Ohio. I ought to be back there, teaching my classes, stopping at Hartnett's Drug Store for a soft drink on the way home, but I am here in a ship fleeing through the stars . . .

His head was spinning and he was afraid that he was going to go out again. He found himself at the door and slid it open and fell rather than walked inside. He heard a startled voice.

This was a bigger room. There was a table whose top was translucent and which showed a bewildering mass of fleeting symbols in bright light, ever changing. There was a screen on one wall of the room and that showed nothing, a blank, dark surface.

Vaillant and Paula Ray and a tall, tough-looking man of middle age were around the table and had looked up, surprised.

Vaillant's face flashed irritation. "Paula, you were supposed to keep him in his cabin!"

"I didn't think he was strong enough to follow," she said.

"I'm not," said Kieran, and pitched over.

The tall middle-aged man reached and caught him before he hit the floor, and eased him into a chair.

He heard, as though from a great distance, Vaillant's voice saying irritatedly, "Let Paula take care of him, Webber. Look at this — we're going to cross another rift —"

There were a few minutes then when everything was very jumbled up in Kieran's mind. The woman was talking to him. She was telling him that they had prepared him physically, as well as psychologically, for the shock of revival, and that he would be quite all right but had to take things more slowly.

He heard her voice but paid little attention. He sat in the chair and blankly watched the two men who hung over the table and its flow of brilliant symbols. Vaillant seemed to tighten up more and more as the moments passed, and there was still about him the look of a coiled spring but now the spring seemed to be wound to the breaking-point. Webber, the tall man with the tough face, watched the fleeting symbols and his face was stony.

"Here we go," he muttered, and both he and Vaillant looked up at the blank black screen on the wall.

Kieran looked too. There was nothing. Then, in an instant, the blackness vanished from the screen and it framed a vista of such cosmic, stunning splendor that Kieran could not grasp it.

Stars blazed like high fires across the screen, loops and chains and shining clots of them. This was not too different from the way they had looked from Wheel Five. But what was different was that the starry firmament was partly blotted out by vast rifted ramparts of blackness, ebon cliffs that went up to infinity. Kieran had seen astronomical photographs like this and knew what the blackness was.

Dust. A dust so fine that its percentage of particles in space would be a vacuum, on Earth. But, here where it extended over parsecs of space, it formed a barrier to light. There was a narrow rift here between the titan cliffs of darkness and he — the ship he was in — was fleeing across that rift.

The screen abruptly went black again. Kieran remained sitting and staring at it. That incredible fleeting vision had finally impressed the utter reality of all this upon his mind. They, this ship, were far from Earth — very far, in one of the dust-clouds in which they were trying to lose pursuers. This was real.

" — will have got another fix on us as we crossed, for sure," Vaillant was saying, in a bitter voice. "They'll have the net out for us — the pattern will be shaping now and we can't slip through it."

"We can't," said Webber. "The ship can't. But the flitter can, with luck."

They both looked at Kieran. "He's the important one," Webber said. "If a couple of us could get him through —"

"No," said Paula. "We couldn't. As soon as they caught the ship and found the flitter gone, they'd be after him."

"Not to Sako," said Webber. "They'd never figure that we'd take him to Sako."

"Do I have a word in this?" asked Kieran, between his teeth.

"What?" asked Vaillant.

"This. The hell with you all. I'll go no place with you or for you."

He got a savage satisfaction from saying it, he was tired of sitting there like a booby while they discussed him, but he did not get the reaction from them he had expected. The two men merely continued to look thoughtfully at him. The woman sighed.

"You see? There wasn't time enough to explain it to him. It's natural for him to react with hostility."

"Put him out, and take him along," said Webber.

"No," said Paula sharply. "If he goes out right now he's liable to stay out. I won't answer for it."

"Meanwhile," said Vaillant with an edge to his voice, "the pattern is forming up. Have you any suggestions, Paula?"

She nodded. "This."

She suddenly squeezed something under Kieran's nose, a small thing that she had produced from her pocket without his noticing it, in his angry preoccupation with the two men. He smelled a sweet, refreshing odor and he struck her arm away.

"Oh, no, you're not giving me any more dopes —" Then he stopped, for suddenly it all seemed wryly humorous to him. "A bunch of bloody incompetents," he said, and laughed. "This is the one thing I would never have dreamed — that a man could sleep, and wake up in a starship, and find the starship manned by blunderers."

"Euphoric," said Paula, to the two men.

"At that," said Webber sourly, "there may be something in what he says about us."

Vaillant turned on him and said fiercely, "If that's what you think —" Then he controlled himself and said tightly, "Quarrelling's no good. We're in a box but we can maybe still put it over if we get this man to Sako. Webber, you and Paula take him in the flitter."

Kieran rose to his feet. "Fine," he said gaily. "Let us go in the flitter, whatever that is. I am already bored with starships."

He felt good, very good. He felt a little drunk, not enough to impede his mental processes but enough to give him a fine devil-may-care indifference to what happened next. So it was only the spray Paula had given him — it still made his body feel better and removed his shock and worry and made everything seem suddenly rather amusing.

"Let us to Sako in the flitter," he said. "After all, I'm living on velvet, I might as well see the whole show. I'm sure that Sako, wherever it is, will be just as full of human folly as Earth was."

"He's euphoric," Paula said again, but her face was stricken.

"Of all the people in that space-cemetery, we had to pick one who thinks like that," said Vaillant, with a sort of restrained fury.

"You said yourself that the oldest one would be the best," said Webber. "Sako will change him."

Kieran walked down the corridor with Webber and Paula and he laughed as he walked. They had brought him back from nothingness without his consent, violating the privacy of death or near-death, and now something that he had just said had bitterly disappointed them.

"Come along," he said buoyantly to the two. "Let us not lag. Once aboard the flitter and the girl is mine."

"Oh for God's sake shut up," said Webber.

4.

IT WAS ridiculous to be flying the stars with a bad hangover, but Kieran had one. His head ached dully, he had an unpleasant metallic taste in his mouth, and his former ebullience had given way to a dull depression. He looked sourly around.

He sat in a confined little metal coop of a cabin, hardly enough in which to stand erect. Paula Ray, in a chair a few feet away was sleeping, her head on her breast. Webber sat forward, in what appeared to be a pilot-chair with a number of crowded control banks in front of it. He was not doing anything to the controls. He looked as though he might be sleeping, too.

That was all — a tiny metal room, blank metal walls, silence. They were, presumably, flying between the stars at incredible speeds but there was nothing to show it. There were no screens such as the one he had seen in the ship, to show by artful scanning devices what vista of suns and darknesses lay outside.

"A flitter," Webber had informed him, "just doesn't have room for the complicated apparatus that such scanners require. Seeing is a luxury you dispense with in a flitter. We'll see when we get to Sako."

After a moment he had added, "If we get to Sako."

Kieran had merely laughed then, and had promptly gone to sleep. When he had awakened, it had been with the euphoria all gone and with his present hangover.

"At least," he told himself, "I can truthfully say that this one wasn't my fault. That blasted spray —"

He looked resentfully at the sleeping woman in the chair. Then he reached and roughly shook her shoulder.

She opened her eyes and looked at him, first sleepily and then with resentment.

"You had no right to wake me up," she said.

Then, before Kieran could retort, she seemed to realize the monumental irony of what she had just said, and she burst into laughter.

"I'm sorry," she said. "Go ahead and say it. I had no right to wake *you* up."

"Let's come back to that," said Kieran after a moment. "Why did you?"

Paula looked at him ruefully. "What I need now is a ten-volume history of the last century, and time enough for you to read it. But since we don't have either —" She broke off, then after a pause asked, "Your date was 1981, wasn't it? It and your name were on the tag of your pressure-suit."

"That's right."

"Well, then. Back in 1981, it was expected that men would spread out to the stars, wasn't it?"

Kieran nodded. "As soon as they had a workable high-speed drive. Several drives were being experimented with even then."

"One of them — the Flournoy principle — was finally made workable," she said. She frowned. "I'm trying to give you this briefly and I keep straying into details."

"Just tell me why you woke me up."

"I'm *trying* to tell you." She asked candidly, "Were you always so damned hateful or did the revivification process do this to you?"

Kieran grinned. "All right. Go ahead."

"Things happened pretty much as people foresaw back in 1981," she said. "The drive was perfected. The ships went out to the nearer stars. They found worlds. They established colonies from the overflowing population of Earth. They found human indigenous races on a few worlds, all of them at a rather low technical level, and they taught them.

"There was a determination from the beginning to make it one universe. No separate nationalistic groups, no chance of wars. The governing council was set up at Altair Two. Every world was represented. There are twenty-nine of them, now. It's expected to go on like that, till there are twenty-nine hundred starworlds represented there, twenty-nine thousand — any number. But —"

Kieran had been listening closely. "But what? What upset this particular utopia?"

"Sako."

"This world we're going to?"

"Yes," she said soberly. "Men found something different about this world when they reached it. It had people — human people — on it, very low in the scale of civilization."

"Well, what was the problem? Couldn't you start teaching them as you had others?"

She shook her head. "It would take a long while. But that wasn't the real problem. It was — You see, there's another race on Sako beside the human ones, and it's a fairly civilized race. The Sakae. The trouble is — the Sakae aren't human."

Kieran stared at her. "So what? If they're intelligent —"

"You talk as though it was the simplest thing in the world," she flashed.

"Isn't it? If your Sakae are intelligent and the humans of Sako aren't, then the Sakae have the rights on that world, don't they?"

She looked at him, not saying anything, and again she had that stricken look of one who has tried and failed. Then from up forward, without turning, Webber spoke.

"What do you think now of Vaillant's fine idea, Paula?"

"It can still work," she said, but there was no conviction in her voice.

"If you don't mind," said Kieran, with an edge to his voice, "I'd still like to know what this Sako business has to do with reviving me."

"The Sakae rule the humans on that world," Paula answered. "There are some of us who don't believe they should. In the Council, we're known as the Humanity Party, because we believe that humans should not be ruled by non-humans."

Again, Kieran was distracted from his immediate question — this time by the phrase "Non-human".

"These Sakae — what are they like?"

"They're not monsters, if that's what you're thinking of," Paula said. "They're bipeds — lizardoid rather than humanoid — and are a fairly intelligent and law-abiding lot."

"If they're all that, and higher in development than the humans, why shouldn't they rule their own world?" demanded Kieran.

Webber uttered a sardonic laugh. Without turning he asked, "Shall I change course and go to Altair?"

"No!" she said. Her eyes flashed at Kieran and she spoke almost breathlessly. "You're very sure about things you just heard about, aren't you? You know what's right and you know what's wrong, even though you've only been in this time, this universe, for a few hours!"

Kieran looked at her closely. He thought he was beginning to get a glimmer of the shape of things now.

"You — all you who woke me up illegally — you belong to this Humanity Party, don't you? You did it for some reason connected with that?"

"Yes," she answered defiantly. "We need a symbol in this political struggle. We thought that one of the oldtime space pioneers, one of the humans who began the conquest of the stars, would be it. We —"

Kieran interrupted. "I think I get it. It was really considerate of you. You drag a man back from what amounts to death, for a party rally. 'Oldtime space hero condemns non-humans' — it would go something like that, wouldn't it?"

"Listen — ," she began.

"Listen, hell," he said. He was hot with rage, shaking with it. "I am glad to say that you could not possibly have picked a worse symbol than me. I have no more use for the idea of the innate sacred superiority of one species over another than I had for that of one kind of man over another."

Her face changed. From an angry woman, she suddenly became a professional psychologist, coolly observing reactions.

"It's not the political question you really resent," she said. "You've wakened to a strange world and you're afraid of it, in spite of all the pre-awakening preparation we gave your subconscious. You're afraid, and so you're angry."

Kieran got a grip on himself. He shrugged. "What you say may be true. But it doesn't change the way I feel. I will not help you one damned bit."

Webber got up from his seat and came back toward them, his tall form stooping. He looked at Kieran and then at the woman.

"We have to settle this right now," he said. "We're getting near enough to Sako to go out of drive. Are we going to land or aren't we?"

"Yes," said Paula steadily. "We're landing."

Webber glanced again at Kieran's face. "But if that's the way he feels —"

"Go ahead and land," she said.

5.

IT WAS nothing like landing in a rocket. First there was the business referred to as "going out of drive". Paula made Kieran strap in and she said, "You may find this unpleasant, but just sit tight. It doesn't last long." Kieran sat stiff and glowering, prepared for anything and determined not to show it no matter how he felt. Then Webber did something to the control board and the universe fell apart. Kieran's stomach came up and stuck in his throat. He was falling — up? Down? Sideways? He didn't know, but whichever it was not all the parts of him were falling at the same rate, or perhaps it was not all in the same direction, he didn't know that either, but it was an exceptionally hideous feeling. He opened his mouth to protest, and all of a sudden he was sitting normally in the chair in the normal cabin and screaming at the top of his lungs.

He shut up.

Paula said, "I told you it would be unpleasant."

"So you did," said Kieran. He sat, sweating. His hands and feet were cold.

Now for the first time he became aware of motion. The flitter seemed to hurtle forward at comet-like speed. Kieran knew that this was merely an ironic little joke, because now they were proceeding at something in the range of normal velocity, whereas before their speed had been quite beyond his comprehension. But he could comprehend this. He could feel it. They were going like a bat out of hell, and somewhere ahead of them was a planet, and he was closed in, blind, a mouse in a nose-cone. His insides writhed with helplessness and the imminence of a crash. He wanted very much to start screaming again, but Paula was watching him.

In a few moments that desire became academic. A whistling shriek began faintly outside the hull and built swiftly to a point where nothing could have been heard above it. Atmosphere. And somewhere under the blind wall of the flitter a rock-hard world-face reeling and rushing, leaping to meet them —

The flitter slowed. It seemed to hang motionless, quivering faintly. Then it dropped. Express elevator in the world's tallest building, top to bottom — only the elevator is a bubble and the wind is tossing it from side to side as it drops and there is no bottom.

They hung again, bounding lightly on the unseen wind.

Then down.

And hang again.

And down.

Paula said suddenly, "Webber. Webber, I think he's dying." She began to unstrap.

Kieran said faintly, "Am I turning green?"

She looked at him, frowning. "Yes."

"A simple old malady. I'm seasick. Tell Webber to quit playing humming-bird and put this thing down."

Paula made an impatient gesture and tightened her belt again.

Hang and drop. Once more, twice more. A little rocking bounce, a light thump, motion ceased. Webber turned a series of switches. Silence.

Kieran said, "Air?"

Webber opened a hatch in the side of the cabin. Light poured in. It had to be sunlight, Kieran knew, but it was a queer color, a sort of tawny orange that carried a pleasantly burning heat. He got loose with Paula helping him and tottered to the hatch. The air smelled of clean sun-warmed dust and some kind of vegetation. Kieran climbed out of the flitter, practically throwing himself out in his haste. He wanted solid ground under him, he didn't care whose or where.

And as his boots thumped onto the red-ochre sand, it occurred to him that it had been a very long time since he had had solid ground underfoot. A very long time indeed —

His insides knotted up again, and this time it was not seasickness but fear, and he was cold all through again in spite of the hot new sun.

He was afraid, not of the present, nor of the future, but of the past. He was afraid of the thing tagged Reed Kieran, the stiff blind voiceless thing wheeling its slow orbit around the Moon, companion to dead worlds and dead space, brother to the cold and the dark.

He began to tremble.

Paula shook him. She was talking but he couldn't hear her. He could only hear the rush of eternal darkness past his ears, the thin squeak of his shadow brushing across the stars. Webber's face was somewhere above him, looking angry and disgusted. He was talking to Paula, shaking his head. They were far away. Kieran was losing them, drifting away from them on the black tide. Then suddenly there was something like an explosion, a crimson flare across the black, a burst of heat against the cold. Shocked and wild, the physical part of him clawed back to reality.

Something hurt him, something threatened him. He put his hand to his cheek and it came away red.

Paula and Webber were yanking at him, trying to get him to move.

A stone whizzed past his head. It struck the side of the flitter with a sharp clack, and fell. Kieran's nervous relays finally connected. He jumped for the open hatch. Automatically he pushed Paula ahead of him, trying to shield her, and she gave him an odd startled look. Webber was already inside. More stones rattled around and one grazed Kieran's thigh. It hurt. His cheek was bleeding freely. He rolled inside the flitter and turned to look back out the hatch. He was mad.

"Who's doing it?" he demanded.

Paula pointed. At first Kieran was distracted by the strangeness of the landscape. The flitter crouched in a vastness of red-ochre sand laced with some low-growing plant that shone like metallic gold in the sunlight. The sand receded in tilted planes lifting gradually to a range of mountains on the right, and dropping gradually to infinity on the left. Directly in front of the flitter and quite literally a stone's throw away was the beginning of a thick belt of trees that grew beside a river, apparently quite a wide one though he could not see much but a tawny sparkling of water. The course of the river could be traced clear back to the mountains by the winding line of woods that followed its bed. The trees themselves were not like any Kieran had seen before. There seemed to be several varieties, all grotesque in shape and exotic in color. There were even some green ones, with long sharp leaves that looked like spearheads.

Exotic or not, they made perfectly adequate cover. Stones came whistling out of the woods, but Kieran could not see anything where Paula was pointing but an occasional shaking of foliage.

"Sakae?" he asked.

Webber snorted. "You'll know it when the Sakae find us. They don't throw stones."

"These are the humans," Paula said. There was an indulgent softness in her voice that irritated Kieran.

"I thought they were our dear little friends," he said.

"You frightened them."

"*I* frightened them?"

"They've seen the flitter before. But they're extremely alert to modes of behavior, and they knew you weren't acting right. They thought you were sick."

"So they tried to kill me. Nice fellows."

"Self-preservation," Webber said. "They can't afford the luxury of too much kindness."

"They're very kind among themselves," Paula said defensively.

To Kieran she added, "I doubt if they were trying to kill you. They just wanted to drive you away."

"Oh, well," said Kieran, "in that case I wouldn't dream of disappointing them. Let's go."

Paula glared at him and turned to Webber. "Talk to them."

"I hope there's time," Webber grunted, glancing at the sky. "We're sitting ducks here. Keep your patient quiet — any more of that moaning and flopping and we're sunk."

He picked up a large plastic container and moved closer to the door.

Paula looked at Kieran's cheek. "Let me fix that."

"Don't bother," he said. At this moment he hoped the Sakae, whoever and whatever they were, would come along and clap these two into some suitable place for the rest of their lives.

Webber began to "talk".

Kieran stared at him, fascinated. He had expected words — primitive words, perhaps resembling the click-speech of Earth's stone-age survivals, but words of some sort. Webber hooted. It was a soft reassuring sound, repeated over and over, but it was not a word. The rattle of stones diminished, then stopped. Webber continued to make his hooting call. Presently it was answered. Webber turned and nodded at Paula, smiling. He reached into the plastic container and drew forth a handful of brownish objects that smelled to Kieran like dried fruit. Webber tossed these out onto the sand. Now he made a different sound, a grunting and whuffling. There was a silence. Webber made the sound again.

On the third try the people came out of the woods.

In all there were perhaps twenty-five of them. They came slowly and furtively, moving a step or two at a time, then halting and peering, prepared to run. The able-bodied men came first, with one in the lead, a fine-looking chap in early middle age who was apparently the chief. The women, the old men, and the children followed, trickling gradually out of the shadow of the trees but remaining where they could disappear in a flash if alarmed. They were all perfectly naked, tall and slender and large-eyed, their muscles strung for speed and agility rather than massive strength. Their bodies gleamed a light bronze color in the sun, and Kieran noticed that the men were beardless and smooth-skinned. Both men and women had long hair, ranging in color from black to tawny, and very clean and glistening. They were a beautiful people, as deer are a beautiful people, graceful, innocent, and wild. The men came to the dried fruits which had been scattered for them. They picked them up and sniffed them, bit them, then began to eat, repeating the grunt-andwhuffle call. The women and children and old men decided every-thing was safe and joined them. Webber tossed out more fruit, and then got out himself, carrying the plastic box.

"What does he do next?" whispered Kieran to Paula. "Scratch their ears? I used to tame squirrels this way when I was a kid."

"Shut up," she warned him. Webber beckoned and she nudged him to move out of the flitter. "Slow and careful."

Kieran slid out of the flitter. Big glistening eyes swung to watch him. The eating stopped. Some of the little ones scuttled for the trees. Kieran froze. Webber hooted and whuffled some more and the tension relaxed. Kieran approached the group with Paula. There was suddenly no truth in what he was doing. He was an actor in a bad scene, mingling with impossible characters in an improb-able setting. Webber making ridiculous noises and tossing his dried fruit around like a caricature of somebody sowing, Paula with her brisk professionalism all dissolved in misty-eyed fondness, himself an alien in this time and place, and these perfectly normal-ap-pearing people behaving like orang-utans with their fur shaved off. He started to laugh and then thought better of it. Once started, he might not be able to stop.

"Let them get used to you," said Webber softly.

Paula obviously had been here before. She had begun to make noises too, a modified hooting more like a pigeon's call. Kieran just stood still. The people moved in around them, sniffing, touching. There was no conversation, no laughing or giggling even among the little girls. A particularly beautiful young woman stood just behind the chief, watching the strangers with big yellow cat-eyes. Kieran took her to be the man's daughter. He smiled at her. She continued to stare, deadpan and blank-eyed, with no answering flicker of a smile. It was as though she had never seen one before. Kieran shivered. All this silence and unresponsiveness became eerie.

"I'm happy to tell you," he murmured to Paula, "that I don't think much of your little pets?"

She could not allow herself to be sharply angry. She only said, in a whisper, "They are not pets, they are not animals. They —"

She broke off. Something had come over the naked people. Every head had lifted, every eye had turned away from the strangers. They were listening. Even the littlest ones were still.

Kieran could not hear anything except the wind in the trees.

"What — ?" he started to ask.

Webber made an imperative gesture for silence. The tableau held for a brief second longer. Then the brown-haired man who seemed to be the leader made a short harsh noise. The people turned and vanished into the trees.

"The Sakae," Webber said. "Get out of sight." He ran toward the flitter. Paula grabbed Kieran's sleeve and pushed him toward the trees.

"What's going on?" he demanded as he ran.

"Their ears are better than ours. There's a patrol ship coming, I think."

The shadows took them in, orange-and-gold-splashed shadows under strange trees. Kieran looked back. Webber had been inside the flitter. Now he tumbled out of the hatch and ran toward them. Behind him the hatch closed and the flitter stirred and then took off all by itself, humming.

"They'll follow it for a while," Webber panted. "It may give us a chance to get away." He and Paula started after the running people.

Kieran balked. "I don't know why I'm running away from anybody."

Webber pulled out a snub-nosed instrument that looked enough like a gun to be very convincing. He pointed it at Kieran's middle.

"Reason one," he said. "If the Sakae catch Paula and me here we're in very big trouble. Reason two — this is a closed area, and you're with us, so *you* will be in very big trouble." He looked coldly at Kieran. "The first reason is the one that interests me most."

Kieran shrugged. "Well, now I know." He ran.

Only then did he hear the low heavy thrumming in the sky.

6.

THE SOUND came rumbling very swiftly toward them. It was a completely different sound from the humming of the flitter, and it seemed to Kieran to hold a note of menace. He stopped in a small clearing where he might see up through the trees. He wanted a look at this ship or flier or whatever it was that had been built and was flown by non-humans.

But Webber shoved him roughly on into a clump of squat trees that were the color of sherry wine, with flat thick leaves.

"Don't move," he said.

Paula was hugging a tree beside him. She nodded to him to do as Webber said.

"They have very powerful scanners." She pointed with her chin. "Look. They've learned."

The harsh warning barks of the men sounded faintly, then were hushed. Nothing moved, except by the natural motion of the wind. The people crouched among the trees, so still that Kieran would not have seen them if he had not known they were there.

The patrol craft roared past, cranking up speed as it went. Webber grinned. "They'll be a couple of hours at least, overhauling and examining the flitter. By that time it'll be dark, and by morning we'll be in the mountains."

The people were already moving. They headed upstream, going at a steady, shuffling trot. Three of the women, Kieran noticed, had babies in their arms. The older children ran beside their mothers. Two of the men and several of the women were white-haired. They ran also.

"Do you like to see them run?" asked Paula, with a sharp note of passion in her voice. "Does it look good to you?"

"No," said Kieran, frowning. He looked in the direction in which the sound of the patrol craft was vanishing.

"Move along," Webber said. "They'll leave us far enough behind as it is."

*****

Kieran followed the naked people through the woods, beside the tawny river. Paula and Webber jogged beside him. The shadows were long now, reaching out across the water.

Paula kept glancing at him anxiously, as though to detect any sign of weakness on his part. "You're doing fine," she said. "You should. Your body was brought back to normal strength and tone, before you ever were awakened."

"They'll slow down when it's dark, anyway," said Webber.

The old people and the little children ran strongly.

"Is their village there?" Kieran asked, indicating the distant mountains.

"They don't live in villages," Paula said. "But the mountains are safer. More places to hide."

"You said this was a closed area. What is it, a hunting preserve?"

"The Sakae don't hunt them any more."

"But they used to?"

"Well," Webber said, "a long time ago. Not for food, the Sakae are vegetarians, but —"

"But," said Paula, "they were the dominant race, and the people were simply beasts of the field. When they competed for land and food the people were hunted down or driven out." She swung an expressive hand toward the landscape beyond the trees. "Why do you think they live in this desert, scraping a miserable existence along the watercourses? It's land the Sakae didn't want. Now, of course, they have no objection to setting it aside as a sort of game preserve. The humans are protected, the Sakae tell us. They're living their natural life in their natural environment, and when we demand that a program be —"

She was out of breath and had to stop, panting. Webber finished for her.

"We want them taught, lifted out of this naked savagery. The Sakae say it's impossible."

"Is it true?" asked Kieran.

"No," said Paula fiercely. "It's a matter of pride. They want to keep their dominance, so they simply won't admit that the people are anything more than animals, and they won't give them a chance to be anything more."

There was no more talking after that, but even so the three out-landers grew more and more winded and the people gained on them. The sun went down in a blaze of blood-orange light that tinted the trees in even more impossible colors and set the river briefly on fire. Then night came, and just after the darkness shut down the patrol craft returned, beating up along the winding river bed. Kieran froze under the black trees and the hair lifted on his skin. For the first time he felt like a hunted thing. For the first time he felt a personal anger.

The patrol craft drummed away and vanished. "They won't come back until daylight," Webber said.

He handed out little flat packets of concentrated food from his pockets. They munched as they walked. Nobody said anything. The wind, which had dropped at sundown, picked up from a different quarter and began to blow again. It got cold. After a while they caught up with the people, who had stopped to rest and eat. The babies and old people for whom Kieran had felt a worried pity were in much better shape than he. He drank from the river and then sat down. Paula and Webber sat beside him, on the ground. The wind blew hard from the desert, dry and chill. The trees thrashed overhead. Against the pale glimmer of the water Kieran could see naked bodies moving along the river's edge, wading, bending, grubbing in the mud. Apparently they found things, for he could see that they were eating. Somewhere close by other people were stripping fruit or nuts from the trees. A man picked up a stone and pounded something with a cracking noise, then dropped the stone again. They moved easily in the dark, as though they were used to it. Kieran recognized the leader's yellow-eyed daughter, her beautiful slender height outlined against the pale-gleaming water. She stood up to her ankles in the soft mud, holding something tight in her two hands, eating.

The sweat dried on Kieran. He began to shiver.

"You're sure that patrol ship won't come back?" he asked.

"Not until they can see what they're looking for."

"Then I guess it's safe." He began to scramble around, feeling for dried sticks.

"What are you doing?"

"Getting some firewood."

"No." Paula was beside him in an instant, her hand on his arm, "No, you mustn't do that."

"But Webber said —"

"It isn't the patrol ship, Kieran. It's the people. They —"

"They what?"

"I told you they were low on the social scale. This is one of the basic things they have to be taught. Right now they still regard fire as a danger, something to run from."

"I see," Kieran said, and let the kindling fall. "Very well, if I can't have a fire, I'll have you. Your body will warm me." He pulled her into his arms.

She gasped, more in astonishment, he thought, than alarm. "What are you talking about?"

"That's a line from an old movie. From a number of old movies, in fact. Not bad, eh?"

He held her tight. She was definitely female. After a moment he pushed her away.

"That was a mistake. I want to be able to go on disliking you without any qualifying considerations."

She laughed, a curiously flat little sound. "Was everybody crazy in your day?" she asked. And then, "Reed —"

It was the first time she had used his given name. "What?"

"When they threw the stones, and we got back into the flitter, you pushed me ahead of you. You were guarding me. Why?"

He stared at her, or rather at the pale blur of her standing close to him. "Well, it's always been sort of the custom for the men to — But now that I think of it, Webber didn't bother."

"No," said Paula. "Back in your day women were still taking advantage of the dual standard — demanding complete equality with men but clinging to their special status. We've got beyond that."

"Do you like it? Beyond, I mean."

"Yes," she said. "It was good of you to do that, but —"

Webber said, "They're moving again. Come on."

The people walked this time, strung out in a long line between the trees and the water, where the light was a little better and the way more open. The three outlanders tagged behind, clumsy in their boots and clothing. The long hair of the people blew in the wind and their bare feet padded softly, light and swift.

Kieran looked up at the sky. The trees obscured much of it so that all he could see was some scattered stars overhead. But he thought that somewhere a moon was rising.

He asked Paula and she said, "Wait. You'll see."

Night and the river rolled behind them. The moonlight became brighter, but it was not at all like the moonlight Kieran remembered from long ago and far away. That had had a cold tranquility to it, but this light was neither cold nor tranquil. It seemed somehow to shift color, too, which made it even less adequate for seeing than the white moonlight he was used to. Sometimes as it filtered through the trees it seemed, ice-green, and again it was reddish or amber, or blue.

They came to a place where the river made a wide bend and they cut across it, clear of the trees. Paula touched Kieran's arm and pointed. "Look."

Kieran looked, and then he stopped still. The light was not moonlight, and its source was not a moon. It was a globular cluster of stars, hung in the sky like a swarm of fiery bees, a burning and pulsing of many colors, diamond-white and gold, green and crimson, peacock blue and smoky umber. Kieran stared, and beside him Paula murmured, "I've been on a lot of planets, but none of them have anything like this."

The people moved swiftly on, paying no attention at all to the sky.

Reluctantly Kieran followed them into the obscuring woods. He kept looking at the open sky above the river, waiting for the cluster to rise high so he could see it.

It was some time after this, but before the cluster rose clear of the trees, that Kieran got the feeling that something, or someone, was following them.

7.

HE HAD stopped to catch his breath and shake an accumulation of sand out of his boots. He was leaning against a tree with his back to the wind, which meant that he was facing their back-trail, and he thought he saw a shadow move where there was nothing to cast a shadow. He straightened up with the little trip-hammers of alarm beating all over him, but he could see nothing more. He thought he might have been mistaken. Just the same, he ran to catch up with the others.

The people were moving steadily. Kieran knew that their senses were far keener than his, and they were obviously not aware of any danger other than the basic one of the Sakae. He decided that he must have been seeing things.

But an uneasiness persisted. He dropped behind again, this time on purpose, after they had passed a clearing. He stayed hidden behind a tree-trunk and watched. The cluster-light was bright now but very confusing to the eye. He heard a rustling that he did not think was wind, and he thought that something started to cross the clearing and then stopped, as though it had caught his scent.

Then he thought that he heard rustlings at both sides of the clearing, stealthy sounds of stalking that closed in toward him. Only the wind, he told himself, but again he turned to run. This time he met Paula, coming back to look for him.

"Reed, are you all right?" she asked. He caught her arm and pulled her around and made her run. "What is it? What's the matter?"

"I don't know." He hurried with her until he could see Webber ahead, and beyond him the bare backs and blowing hair of the people. "Listen," he said, "are there any predators here?"

"Yes," Paula said, and Webber turned sharply around.

"Have you seen something?"

"I don't know. I thought I did. I'm not sure."

"Where?"

"Behind us."

Webber made the harsh barking danger call, and the people stopped. Webber stood looking back the way they had come. The women caught the children and the men fell back to where Webber stood. They looked and listened, sniffing the air. Kieran listened too, but now he did not hear any rustlings except the high thrashing of the branches. Nothing stirred visibly and the wind would carry away any warning scent.

The men turned away. The people moved on again. Webber shrugged.

"You must have been mistaken, Kieran."

"Maybe. Or maybe they just can't think beyond the elementary. If they don't smell it, it isn't there. If something is after us it's coming up-wind, the way any hunting animal works. A couple of the men ought to circle around and —"

"Come on," said Webber wearily.

They followed the people beside the river. The cluster was high now, a hive of suns reflected in the flowing water, a kaleidoscopic rippling of colors.

Now the women were carrying the smaller children. The ones too large to be carried were lagging behind a little. So were the aged. Not much, yet. Kieran, conscious that he was weaker than the weakest of these, looked ahead at the dim bulk of the mountains and thought that they ought to be able to make it. He was not at all sure that he would.

The river made another bend. The trail lay across the bend, clear of the trees. It was a wide bend, perhaps two miles across the neck. Ahead, where the trail joined the river again, there was a rocky hill. Something about the outlines of the hill seemed wrong to Kieran, but it was too far away to be sure of anything. Overhead the cluster burned gloriously. The people set out across the sand.

Webber looked back. "You see?" he said. "Nothing."

They went on. Kieran was beginning to feel very tired now, all the artificial strength that had been pumped into him before his awakening was running out. Webber and Paula walked with their heads down, striding determinedly but without joy.

"What do you think now?" she asked Kieran. "Is this any way for humans to live?"

The ragged line of women and children moved ahead of them, with the men in the lead. It was not natural, Kieran thought, for children to be able to travel so far, and then he remembered that the young of non-predacious species have to be strong and fleet at an early age.

Suddenly one of the women made a harsh, shrill cry.

Kieran looked where she was looking, off to the left, to the river and the curving line of trees. A large black shadow slipped across the sand. He looked behind him. There were other shadows, coming with long easy bounds out of the trees, fanning out in a shallow crescent. They reminded Kieran of some animal he had once seen in a zoo, a partly catlike, partly doglike beast, a cheetah he thought it had been called, only the cheetah was spotted like a leopard and these creatures were black, with stiff, upstanding ears. They bayed, and the coursing began.

"Nothing," said Kieran bitterly. "I count seven."

Webber said, "My God, I —"

*****

The people ran. They tried to break back to the river and the trees that could be climbed to safety, but the hunters turned them. Then they fled blindly forward, toward the hill. They ran with all their strength, making no sound. Kieran and Webber ran with them, with Paula between them. Webber seemed absolutely appalled.

"Where's that gun you had?" Kieran panted.

"It's not a gun, only a short-range shocker," he said. "It wouldn't stop these things. Look at them!"

They bounded, sporting around them, howling with a sound like laughter. They were as large as leopards and their eyes glowed in the cluster-light. They seemed to be enjoying themselves, as though hunting was the most delightful game in the world. One of them ran up to within two feet of Kieran and snapped at him with its great jaws, dodging agilely when he raised his arm. They drove the people, faster and faster. At first the men had formed around the women and children. But the formation began to disintegrate as the weaker ones dropped behind, and no attempt was made to keep it. Panic was stronger than instinct now. Kieran looked ahead. "If we can make it to that hill —"

Paula screamed and he stumbled over a child, a girl about five, crawling on her hands and knees. He picked her up. She bit and thrashed and tore at him, her bare little body hard as whalebone and slippery with sweat. He could not hold onto her. She kicked herself free of his hands and rushed wildly out of reach, and one of the black hunters pounced in and bore her away, shrieking thinly like a fledgling bird in the jaws of a cat.

"Oh my God," said Paula, and covered her head with her arms, trying to shut out sight and sound. He caught her and said harshly, "Don't faint, because I can't carry you." The child's mother, whichever of the women it might have been, did not look back.

An old woman who strayed aside was pulled down and dragged off, and then one of the white-haired men. The hill was closer. Kieran saw now what was wrong with it. Part of it was a building. He was too tired and too sick to be interested, except as it offered a refuge. He spoke to Webber, with great difficulty because he was winded. And then he realized that Webber wasn't there.

*****

Webber had stumbled and fallen. He had started to get up, but the hunters were on him. He was on his hands and knees facing them, screaming at them to get away from him. He had, obviously, had little or no experience with raw violence. Kieran ran back to him, with Paula close behind.

"Use your gun!" he yelled. He was afraid of the black hunters, but he was full of rage and the rage outweighed the fear. He yelled at them, cursing them. He hurled sand into their eyes, and one that was creeping up on Webber from the side he kicked. The creature drew off a little, not frightened but surprised. They were not used to this sort of thing from humans. "Your gun!" Kieran roared again, and Webber pulled the snub-nosed thing out of his pocket. He stood up and said unsteadily, "I told you, it's not a gun. It won't kill anything. I don't think —"

"Use it," said Kieran. "And get moving again. Slowly."

They started to move, and then across the sky a great iron voice spoke like thunder. "Lie down," it said, "please. Lie down flat."

Kieran turned his head, startled. From the direction of the building on the hill a vehicle was speeding toward them.

"The Sakae," said Webber with what was almost a sob of relief. "Lie down."

As he did so, Kieran saw a pale flash shoot out from the vehicle and knock over a hunter still hanging on the flanks of the fleeing people. He hugged the sand. Something went whining and whistling over him, there was a thunk and a screech. It was repeated, and then the iron voice spoke again.

"You may get up now. Please remain where you are." The vehicle was much closer. They were bathed in sudden light. The voice said, "Mr. Webber, you are holding a weapon. Please drop it."

"It's only a little shocker," Webber said, plaintively. He dropped it.

The vehicle had wide tracks that threw up clouds of sand. It came clanking to a halt. Kieran, shading his eyes, thought he distinguished two creatures inside, a driver and a passenger.

The passenger emerged, climbing with some difficulty over the steep step of the track, his tail rattling down behind him like a length of thick cable. Once on the ground he became quite agile, moving with a sort of oddly graceful prance on his powerful legs. He approached, his attention centered on Kieran. But he observed the amenities, placing one delicate hand on his breast and making a slight bow.

"Doctor Ray." His muzzle, shaped something like a duck's bill, nevertheless formed Paula's name tolerably well. "And you, I think, are Mr. Kieran."

Kieran said, "Yes." The star-cluster blazed overhead. The dead beasts lay behind him, the people with their flying hair had run on beyond his sight. He had been dead for a hundred years and now he was alive again. Now he was standing on alien soil, facing an alien form of life, communicating with it, and he was so dog-tired and every sensory nerve was so thoroughly flayed that he had nothing left to react with. He simply looked at the Saka as he might have looked at a fence-post, and said, "Yes."

The Saka made his formal little bow again. "I am Bregg." He shook his head. "I'm glad I was able to reach you in time. You people don't seem to have any notion of the amount of trouble you make for us —"

Paula, who had not spoken since the child was carried off, suddenly screamed at Bregg, "Murderer!"

She sprang at him, striking him in blind hysteria.

8.

BREGG SIGHED. He caught Paula in those fine small hands that seemed to have amazing strength and held her, at arm's length. "Doctor Ray," he said. He shook her. "Doctor Ray." She stopped screaming. "I don't wish to administer a sedative because then you will say that I drugged you. But I will if I must."

Kieran said, "I'll keep her quiet."

He took her from Bregg. She collapsed against him and began to cry. "Murderers," she whispered. "That little girl, those old people —"

Webber said, "You could exterminate those beasts. You don't have to let them hunt the people like that. It's — it's —"

"Unhuman is the word you want," said Bregg. His voice was exceedingly weary. "Please get into the car."

They climbed in. The car churned around and sped back toward the building. Paula shivered, and Kieran held her in his arms. Webber said after a moment or two, "How did you happen to be here, Bregg?"

"When we caught the flitter and found it empty, it was obvious that you were with the people, and it became imperative to find you before you came to harm. I remembered that the trail ran close by this old outpost building, so I had the patrol ship drop us here with an emergency vehicle."

Kieran said, "You knew the people were coming this way?"

"Of course." Bregg sounded surprised. "They migrate every year at the beginning of the dry season. How do you suppose Webber found them so easily?"

Kieran looked at Webber. He asked, "Then they weren't running from the Sakae?"

"Of course they were," Paula said. "You saw them yourself, cowering under the trees when the ship went over."

"The patrol ships frighten them," Bregg said. "Sometimes to the point of stampeding them, which is why we use them only in emergencies. The people do not connect the ships with us."

"That," said Paula flatly, "is a lie."

Bregg sighed. "Enthusiasts always believe what they want to believe. Come and see for yourself."

She straightened up. "What have you done to them?"

"We've caught them in a trap," said Bregg, "and we are presently going to stick needles into them — a procedure necessitated by your presence, Doctor Ray. They're highly susceptible to imported viruses, as you should remember — one of your little parties of do-gooders succeeded in wiping out a whole band of them not too many years ago. So — inoculations and quarantine."

Lights had blazed up in the area near the building. The car sped toward them.

Kieran said slowly, "Why don't you just exterminate the hunters and have done with them?"

"In your day, Mr. Kieran — yes, I've heard all about you — in your day, did you on Earth exterminate the predators so that their natural prey might live more happily?"

Bregg's long muzzle and sloping skull were profiled against the lights.

"No," said Kieran, "we didn't. But in that case, they were all animals."

"Exactly," said Bregg. "No, wait, Doctor Ray. Spare me the lecture. I can give you a much better reason than that, one even you can't quarrel with. It's a matter of ecology. The number of humans destroyed by these predators annually is negligible but they do themselves destroy an enormous number of small creatures with which the humans compete for their food. If we exterminated the hunters the small animals would multiply so rapidly that the humans would starve to death."

The car stopped beside the hill, at the edge of the lighted area. A sort of makeshift corral of wire fencing had been set up, with wide wings to funnel the people into the enclosure, where a gate was shut on them. Two Sakae were mounting guard as the party from the car approached the corral. Inside the fence Kieran could see the people, flopped around in positions of exhaustion. They did not seem to be afraid now. A few of them were drinking from a supply of water provided for them. There was food scattered for them on the ground.

Bregg said something in his own language to one of the guards, who looked surprised and questioned him, then departed, springing strongly on his powerful legs. "Wait," said Bregg.

They waited, and in a moment or two the guard came back leading one of the black hunting beasts on a chain. It was a female, somewhat smaller than the ones Kieran had fought with, and having a slash of white on the throat and chest. She howled and sprang up on Bregg, butting her great head into his shoulder, wriggling with delight. He petted her, talking to her, and she laughed doglike and licked his cheek.

"They domesticate well," he said. "We've had a tame breed for centuries."

He moved a little closer to the corral, holding tight to the animal's chain. Suddenly she became aware of the people. Instantly the good-natured pet turned into a snarling fury. She reared on her hind legs and screamed, and inside the corral the people roused up. They were not frightened now. They spat and chattered, clawing up sand and pebbles and bits of food to throw through the fence. Bregg handed the chain to the guard, who hauled the animal away by main force.

Paula said coldly, "If your point was that the people are not kind to animals, my answer is that you can hardly blame them."

"A year ago," Bregg said, "some of the people got hold of her two young ones. They were torn to pieces before they could be saved, and she saw it. I can't blame her, either."

He went on to the gate and opened it and went inside. The people drew back from him. They spat at him, too, and pelted him with food and pebbles. He spoke to them, sternly, in the tone of one speaking to unruly dogs, and he spoke words, in his own tongue. The people began to shuffle about uneasily. They stopped throwing things. He stood waiting.

The yellow-eyed girl came sidling forward and rubbed herself against his thigh, head, shoulder and flank. He reached down and stroked her, and she whimpered with pleasure and arched her back.

"Oh, for God's sake," said Kieran, "let's get out of here."

*****

Later, they sat wearily on fallen blocks of cement inside a dusty, shadowy room of the old building. Only a hand-lamp dispelled the gloom, and the wind whispered coldly, and Bregg walked to and fro in his curious prance as he talked.

"It will be a little while before the necessary medical team can be picked up and brought here," he said. "We shall have to wait."

"And then?" asked Kieran.

"First to —" Bregg used a word that undoubtedly named a city of the Sakae but that meant nothing to Kieran, " — and then to Altair Two. This, of course, is a council matter."

He stopped and looked with bright, shrewd eyes at Kieran. "You are quite the sensation already, Mr. Kieran. The whole community of starworlds is already aware of the illegal resuscitation of one of the pioneer spacemen, and of course there is great interest." He paused. "You, yourself, have done nothing unlawful. You cannot very well be sent back to sleep, and undoubtedly the council will want to hear you. I am curious as to what you will say."

"About Sako?" said Kieran. "About — them?" He made a gesture toward a window through which the wind brought the sound of stirring, of the gruntings and whufflings of the corralled people.

"Yes. About them."

"I'll tell you how I feel," Kieran said flatly. He saw Paula and Webber lean forward in the shadows. "I'm a human man. The people out there may be savage, low as the beasts, good for nothing the way they are — but they're human. You Sakae may be intelligent, civilized, reasonable, but you're not human. When I see you ordering them around like beasts, I want to kill you. That's how I feel."

Bregg did not change his bearing, but he made a small sound that was almost a sigh.

"Yes," he said. "I feared it would be so. A man of your times — a man from a world where humans were all-dominant — would feel that way." He turned and looked at Paula and Webber. "It appears that your scheme, to this extent, was successful."

"No, I wouldn't say that," said Kieran.

Paula stood up. "But you just told us how you feel —"

"And it's the truth," said Kieran. "But there's something else." He looked thoughtfully at her. "It was a good idea. It was bound to work — a man of my time was bound to feel just this way you wanted him to feel, and would go away from here crying your party slogans and believing them. But you overlooked something —"

He paused, looking out the window into the sky, at the faint vari-colored radiance of the cluster.

"You overlooked the fact that when you awoke me, I would no longer be a man of my own time — or of any time. I was in darkness for a hundred years — with the stars my brothers, and no man touching me. Maybe that chills a man's feelings, maybe something deep in his mind lives and has time to think. I've told you how I feel, yes. But I haven't told you what I think —"

He stopped again, then said, "The people out there in the corral have my form, and my instinctive loyalty is to them. But instinct isn't enough. It would have kept us in the mud of Earth forever, if it could. Reason took us out to the wider universe. Instinct tells me that those out there are my people. Reason tells me that you —" he looked at Bregg, " — who are abhorrent to me, who would make my skin creep if I touched you, you who go by reason — that you are my real people. Instinct made a hell of Earth for millennia — I say we ought to leave it behind us there in the mud and not let it make a hell of the stars. For you'll run into this same problem over and over again as you go out into the wider universe, and the old parochial human loyalties must be altered, to solve it."

He looked at Paula and said, "I'm sorry, but if anyone asks me, that is what I'll say."

"I'm sorry, too," she said, rage and dejection ringing in her voice. "Sorry we woke you. I hope I never see you again."

Kieran shrugged. "After all, you did wake me. You're responsible for me. Here I am, facing a whole new universe, and I'll need you." He went over and patted her shoulder.

"Damn you," she said. But she did not move away from him.

THE MONSTERS
OF JUNTONHEIM

CHAPTER 1

The Rune Key

BRAY CALLED excitedly to me from the forward deck of the schooner.

"Keith, your hunch was right. There's something queer in this trawl!"

Involuntarily I shuddered in the sudden chill of fear. Somehow I had known that the trawl would bring something up from the icy Arctic sea. Pure intuition had made me persuade Bray to lower his trawl in this unpromising spot.

"Coming, Bray!" I called and hurried through the litter of sleds and snarling dogs.

Our schooner, the sturdy auxiliary ice-breaker *Peter Saul*, was lying at anchor in the Lincoln Sea, only four hundred miles south of the Pole. A hundred yards away, the dazzling white fields of ice stretched northward — a vast, frozen, scarcely explored waste.

When we had reached the ice pack the night before, I had somehow conceived the idea that Bray, the oceanographer, ought to try his luck here. Bray had laughed at my hunch at first, but had finally consented.

"Are you psychic, Keith?" he demanded. "Look what the trawl brought up!"

A heavy, ancient-looking gold cylinder, about eight inches long, was sticking out of the frozen mud. On its sides were engraved a row of queer symbols, almost worn away.

"What in the world is it?" I breathed. "And what are those letters on it?"

Halsen, a big, bearded Norwegian sailor, answered me.

"Those letters are in my own language, sir." "Nonsense," I said sharply. "I know Norwegian pretty well. Those letters are not in your language."

"Not the one my people write today," Halsen explained, "but the old Norse — the rune writing. I have seen such writing on old stones in the museum at Oslo."

"Norse runes?" I blurted. "Then this must be damned ancient."

"Let's take it down to Dubman," Bray suggested. "He ought to be able to tell us."

Dubman, the waspish little archaeologist of the expedition, looked up in annoyance from his collection of Eskimo arrowheads when we entered. Angrily he took the cylinder and glared at it.

Instantly his eyes lit up behind the thick spectacles.

"Old Norse!" he exclaimed. "But these are runes of the most ancient form — pre-Valdstenan! What is it?"

"Maybe the runes on it can give us a clue," I said eagerly.

"I'll soon find out what they mean," Dubman declared.

With a magnifying glass, he began to examine the symbols graven on the golden cylinder. Bray and I waited. I felt queerly taut. I could not understand just why I was so excited about this find, but everything about it had been queer. A persistent inner voice had kept telling me: "Make Bray let down his trawl here!" And the first time it was lowered, it had brought up a gold tube that must have lain on the sea-floor for centuries.

"Got it!" Dubman stated, looking up. "This thing is old, all right — the most ancient form of runic. The translation doesn't tell much. Listen to this —

> *Rune key am I,*
> *Chaining dark evil,*
> *Midgard snake, Fenris,*
> *And Loki, arch-devil.*
> *While I lie far,*
> *The Aesir safe are,*
> *Bring me not home,*
> *Lest Ragnarok come."*

A chill rippled through me, as though even the translation of those ancient runes could terrify me. Impatiently I shook off the feeling.

"What does all that stuff about the Aesir and Loki mean?" I asked.

"The Aesir were the ancient Norse gods, eternally youthful and powerful. Ruled by Odin, they lived in the fabled city of Asgard. Loki turned against them. With his two familiars, the monstrous wolf Fenris and the great Midgard serpent, Loki joined the Jotuns, the giant enemies of the gods. The gods finally managed to chain Loki, his wolf and his serpent. But it was predicted that if Loki ever broke his bonds, that would bring about Ragnarok — the doom of the Aesir.

"Bring me not home, lest Ragnarok come," he quoted. "This key claims to be the one with which Loki and his pets were locked up. Probably some ancient Norse priest made it to 'prove' the old myths, was shipwrecked and lost it in the sea."

"I don't get it," Bray complained. "What made you tell me to let down my trawl in just that spot, Keith?"

When I picked up the gold cylinder, a current of queer power ran up my arm. Somehow it seemed to warn me to drop it back into the sea. But I didn't obey, for something alien commanded me to keep the rune key.

"Can I study this for a few days?" I asked abruptly. "I'll take good care of it."

"I didn't know you had archaeological tastes, Masters," Dubman said, astonished. "But you were responsible for finding it, so you can keep it awhile. Don't lose it, though, or I'll skin you."

Through the little ring on one end of the cylinder, I passed a cord and hung it around my neck. It was cold against my skin — cold and menacing, persistently warning . . .

Naturally I tried to convince myself that I just wasn't the superstitious type. Besides my thirty years of disciplining myself to examine even obvious truths, and my towering height of lean muscle, I have inherited the canny skepticism of my Scottish ancestors. Anyhow, a scientist couldn't admit the existence of the supernatural. Like most other physicists, I claimed there were still a lot of forces which science hasn't had time to investigate yet. When it does, there will be no room for superstition, for belief in the supernatural is merely ignorance of natural laws.

But I worked twice as hard as anybody else, unloading our small rocket plane for my first reconnaissance flight northward. Not even intense physical labor could make me forget the sinister cold force of the rune key inside my shirt, though.

The menacing current felt even stronger when I stood on deck that night. Overhead, the aurora borealis pulsated in shifting bars and banners of unearthly radiance, changing the immense frozen ocean from white to green, violet and crimson. Like a mad musician, the freezing wind strummed the schooner's halyards and made the masts boom out their deep voices.

But the rune key under my shirt tormented me with its conflicting demands. It ordered me to throw it back to the icy waters. Helpless, I ripped it out and tugged at the cord, trying to snap it. An even stronger command made me put it back.

The moment I buttoned my shirt, I cursed myself for being a fool. Why should I want to destroy something of potential value to science? Inwardly, though, I realized that the demands of the rune key were stronger than my own will.

"It can be explained scientifically," I muttered uneasily. "Everything has a scientific explanation, once we can isolate it."

But how could a small, golden cylinder penetrate my mind and order it about like a servant? What filled my heart with doubt and dread?

For all my canny skepticism and scientific training, I couldn't answer those insistent questions, nor keep myself from being tormented by the damned thing . . .

CHAPTER II

Mystery Land

IT WAS a brilliant Arctic morning. The sun glittered on the white ice-pack, the placid grey sea and the battered hull of the *Peter Saul*. I was ready for my first reconnaissance flight northward. Doctor John Carrul, chief of the expedition, called down to me from the rail of the schooner.

"Don't go too far the first trip, Masters. And return at once if the weather grows threatening."

"There won't be any storms for days," I replied confidently. "I know Arctic weather."

"You'd better leave that rune key with me," Dubman shrilled. "I'd hate to lose it if you cracked up."

During the past few days, the golden cylinder hadn't been out of my thoughts. Whatever menacing force radiated from the key, it was still far beyond my science. I had tested it with electroscopes, but they registered nothing. Yet it did radiate some disturbing force. It was the same with the mental command that fought the one which tried to make me throw away the key. Apparently supernatural or not, it had to have some rational, mundane explanation.

My obsession with the mystery had made me read Dubman's books on old Norse myths. The Aesir, said the legends, inhabited the fabled city of Asgard, which was separated from the land of Midgard by a deep gulf that was spanned by a wonderful rainbow bridge. All around Midgard lay the frozen, lifeless wastes of Niffle-heim.

In the great hall Valhalla reigned Odin, king of the Aesir, and his wife Frigga. And in other castles dwelt the other gods and goddesses. Once Loki had been of the Aesir, till he turned traitor and was prisoned with his two monstrous pets, the wolf Fenris and the Midgard serpent Iormungandr.

I read about the Jotuns — the giants who lived in dark Jotunheim and incessantly battled the Aesir. Then there were the dwarfs of Earth, the Alfings who dwelt in subterranean Alfheim. Hel, the wicked death-goddess whose dreaded hall was near the dark city of the Jotuns. Muspelheim, the fiery realm beneath Midgard.

One thing in these legends impressed me. They depicted the Aesir as mortal beings who possessed the secret of eternal youth in common with the giants and dwarfs. None of them grew old, but any of them could be slain. If Loki were released, bringing about

Ragnarok — the twilight of the gods — the Aesir would perish.

As I delved deeper into the books of Rydberg, Anderson and Du Chaillu, I learned that ethnologists thought there was some real basis to these legends. They believed the Aesir had been real people with remarkable powers. All my reading had only intensified my interest in the enigmatic rune key from the sea. I knew it bordered on superstition, but I felt that if I were away from the influence of others, the damned thing might actually get coherent.

"I'll be back by four o'clock," I said. "It won't take me long to map a sled route."

"Be sure you take no chances," Dr. Carrul called anxiously.

Streaking across the ice, the rocket plane roared into the chill air. I circled above the schooner, climbed higher, and then headed northward across the ice-pack. Within ten minutes, I was flying over the endless expanse of the frozen Arctic Ocean, warm and snug in the oxygen-filled cabin.

A vast white plain, glittering like diamonds in the sunlight, the sea ice had jammed and split, and there were long leads of open water. My mission was to chart the easiest route toward the Pole, so the sleds would lose no time detouring around leads or scrambling over ridges. Once a weather observation camp was established, I would carry in supplies in the plane.

Hundreds of thousands of square miles of the enormous sea of ice had never been seen by man. Earth's last real home of mystery was dazzlingly beautiful — but it was murderous, terrifying, sinister . . .

Absorbed in keeping the plane on its course and making a map of the ice below, my sense of time was temporarily paralyzed. The rocket motor roared tirelessly, and the ice unrolled endlessly below. When my ship lurched sharply, I abruptly realized that the wind was suddenly rising. I looked around, startled. A huge dark wall was rising across the southern horizon.

"Damn it, I'll never call myself a weather prophet again," I swore. "There just couldn't be any storm. But there it is!"

I banked around sharply and flew southward, fighting to rise above the fury. But the higher I climbed, the higher the black, boiling wall of the storm seemed to rise. I knew I was caught.

"Two minutes to live," I gritted. "It'll be a fast death —"

Driving before it a cloud of stinging snow, the storm smacked my plane like a giant hand. Stunned by the impact, deafened, I swung the nose around and let the wind sweep the plane northward. There was no hope of fighting. I could only run before the gale until its fury subsided. The whole sky was dark and raging around me, filled with screaming wind and snow. Gripping the firing wheel, I battled to keep the reeling plane in the air.

But why did the rune key inside my shirt seem to throb with frantic warning? Why did that alien voice in my mind seem eager and exultant? Why did I feel there was something purposeful about this gale's direction? The storm had come up suddenly out of a clear sky as soon as my plane was well in the air. Now it was hurling me straight in one direction.

The imminent peril of death grew less unnerving than the mounting suspicion that there was something deliberate about the storm. The warning force throbbing from the rune key, and the wildly exultant alien voice in my brain, combined to demoralize me.

After nearly six hours of ceaseless storm-driven flight, I received the greatest shock. Peering ahead through the frosted cabin windows, I realized suddenly that there was a great area dead ahead — which I could not see!

"It can't be real!" I gasped. "A colossal blind spot —"

My vision seemed to slide around that vast area. I could see the ice-pack beyond it, scores of miles away. I could see the ice on either side of it. But the area itself just didn't register.

"Some trick of refraction, perhaps due to the terrestrial magnetic currents that are strong here," I muttered. "Maybe it's connected with the mystery of the aurora."

My scientific reasoning didn't quiet my nerves. For the storm that bore me on was carrying me straight toward that huge blind spot. When I was almost to the edge of the enigmatic area my vision seemed to slide away to either side, almost at right angles. If this was refraction, it was a type that was completely unknown to science.

My storm-tossed plane hurtled with reckless speed toward the edge of the vast blind spot; I could see nothing whatever ahead. Everything seemed crazily twisted out of focus, distorted by that weird wall.

Abruptly the gale flung my reeling plane directly through the fantastic wall that defied my vision — and I was inside the blind spot! But now I could not see outside it.

"This — this is impossible!" I gasped with startled terror.

I could see nothing but the interior, a great space of tossing ocean, curving ominously to every sinister horizon. Black waves, black clouds . . . Suddenly I gasped in amazement. Far ahead loomed a long, high mass of forbidding, dark land.

The storm still howled with all its original fury, carrying me dangerously low over the foam-fanged waves toward the distant land. Through the scudding snow, I detected a faint greenish radiance. But realization of my immediate peril swept away my demoralization. I could not land in that vicious sea. Yet neither could I climb again in that gale.

The land I had glimpsed was now a mile ahead of me, its frowning eastern cliffs stretching right across my course. The gray precipices were hundreds of feet high. Above them, the land ran back into dark forests and shaggy wooded hills where no landing was possible. Then I saw a small beach strewn with boulders. Pure desperation made me head the plane toward it.

Over the boiling white hell of breakers I shot. My wheels touched the beach. Before I could brake with the forward jets, the port window smashed against a projecting boulder. But that was the only damage when I stopped out of reach of the waves.

I shut off the rocket motor and stumbled out of the ship. My knees were trembling with the reaction of prolonged tenseness. But the land and sea inside the incredible blind spot made me forget my exhaustion.

The air was keenly cold. It was the cold of an ordinary northern spring, though, not the bitter polar chill it should have been. The sky was dark with clouds, fleeing before the gale. The boom of raging surf and keen of wailing winds were loud in my ears. Stranger even than the comparative warmth was the faint green radiance that seemed to pervade the air. An eldritch glow that could barely be seen, it seemed to stream upward from the ground. It was oddly exhilarating.

"Might be gamma radiation from some unknown source," I reasoned. "That may account for the refraction that makes this whole area a blind spot. I wish I had instruments here to check. Hope it doesn't have the usual effects of gamma radiation on human tissue. But it seems invigorating."

Excitement began to rise in me. I had found a hidden land of strange warmth completely unknown to civilization, here in the polar wastes. Its strange trick of refraction had defied discovery until now. No scientist could have been dropped in that blind spot without feeling the urge to explore. Waiting for the storm to die down, flying out of the blind area and getting back to the ship for a regular exploration party would have been wiser. But like every other man, I had the desire to be first in an unknown land.

I moored the plane between two boulders and removed my flying togs to don regulation exploring clothes for Arctic weather. With a pack of food pellets and blankets on my back, I began to climb the jagged, craggy wall.

Gasping for breath, I reached the rim of the lofty cliffs. Cold sea winds buffeted me, and the boom of bursting breakers came muf-fledly from below. Harshly screaming sea-gulls soared and circled around me.

To my right lay the edge of the cliffs. To my left, a strip of heather ended in a forest of fir trees, bending in the wind. Beyond the dark fir forest, shaggy, wooded hills rose steeply. Toward the south lay the greater part of the land, rising into higher forested hills. It was a wild northern landscape, bleak, harsh, inhospitable. Yet somehow I relished being alone among screaming winds and gulls, and booming surf, and groaning trees.

I stared at the towering little island I had glimpsed. Its cliffs rose sheer from the green sea for a thousand feet. Its flat top was on a level with the mainland, and separated from it only by a narrow, deep chasm through which the ocean surged.

But upon the island itself rose massed gray towers — buildings! Great castles stood out boldly against the gray, tossing sky, grouped into an amazing city on the small plateau. From the island to the mainland sprang the arch of a stupendous bridge. The flying bow of stone soared up and out for hundreds of feet. Painted in brilliant red and blue and yellow, it gleamed like a fixed rainbow.

A rainbow bridge, leading to the high eyrie of great gray castles! Into my mind rushed the stupefying memory of the legends I had read so recently — Asgard, the fabled city of the Norse gods — the rainbow bridge that connected their abode with Midgard.

Was I looking upon the city of the Aesir? Impossible! Yet this place was real . . .

CHAPTER III

Jotun and Aesir

A CRY in the unhuman uproar startled me. I whirled around. A horse and rider were charging along the edge of the cliff, coming from the south.

"Good Lord!" I gasped. "Must everything be like a dream?"

The rider of that charging black steed was a young woman, but like none I had ever seen before. She wore a winged metal helmet, beneath which her bright yellow hair streamed like flame in the wind. Blue eyes flared hatred out of a beautiful, angry face. Her dress was a gleaming brynja, or coat of ringed mail, over a kirtle. Her white knees were bare, gripping the saddle. As she urged her mount down upon me, a straight, light sword flashed in her hand.

"You dare spy upon Asgard, Jotun dog!" she cried fiercely in a language that was remarkably close to Norwegian. "Death for that!"

Then that high eyrie of great gray castles was Asgard, home of the legendary Aesir! And this wrathful Viking maid took me for a Jotun, one of the race who were mortal enemies of the Aesir! Was I dreaming all this, or had I actually stumbled somehow into the land of ancient Viking legend?

Then I woke to realization of my peril. As the woman's sword stabbed toward my breast, I ducked under it. I felt the blade scream above my head as her horse thundered past. Swiftly I reached up and grabbed her outstretched mail-clad arm. My hold tore her from the saddle.

The sword flew from her grasp as she fell. But she was up and darting toward it in a single motion. I leaped after her and caught her before she could reach the weapon. She fought like a tigress. The strength of her slender, mail-clad body was amazing. Her small fist struck my mouth furiously.

"Scum of Jotunheim!" she hissed. I finally succeeded in pinning her arms to her sides. Her white face, inches away from my own, was blazing with rage, her sea-blue eyes stormy in wild anger. She was beautiful, with a vibrant loveliness like that of a tempest. Her helmeted, golden head came only to my chin, but her blue eyes glared into mine without a trace of fear.

"You'll dangle from the walls of Asgard for daring to lay hands on me, Jotun!" she snapped.

She spoke a strangely antique form of the Norwegian tongue. I answered in the Norwegian I knew.

"Why did you try to kill me?" I asked. "I'm not your enemy."

"You are a Jotun, an enemy to the Aesir," she declared. "You have the dark hair of a true Jotun dog, even though you have chosen to dress in outlandish garments. And you dared spy on Asgard!"

In the old legends, I remembered, the mighty Aesir had been fair-haired. Their mortal enemies, the Jotuns, had been dark-haired.

"I am no Jotun," I said earnestly. "I have but newly come to this land, from far across the outer ice."

She laughed scornfully. "Do you think I believe that you have come from beyond frozen Niffleheim? Your lie is not even clever. Why do you delay in killing me? Death is preferable to your touch, Jotun. And the death of Freya will soon be avenged."

"Freya?" I gasped.

This woman was Freya, whom the old Vikings had worshipped — Freya of the white hands, loveliest of the Aesir? It was impossible! She was real, warm, panting with hate as she sought to free herself. Yet she had spoken of Asgard. That distant eyrie of gray castle was Asgard, just as the legends had described it, even to the flying rainbow bridge that connected it with the mainland.

"I can't understand, Freya," I faltered, still holding her. "My name is Keith Masters. I came from beyond the ice — Niffleheim, as you call it."

For a moment, doubt softened her stony blue eyes. Then she looked past me, and they became bitter and hate-filled again.

"You need lie no longer. Here are your Jotun comrades now, come to help you."

I turned, appalled. Eight men were approaching stealthily, after tethering their horses at the edge of the forest. They were taller even than I. Their hair was black as mine, and hung down in shaggy locks from under cap-like metal helmets. They wore armor tunics of overlapping metal scales, and high buskins on their feet, and carried swords and shields. Their faces were black-bearded, brutal.

"He is the man — kill him!" a brawny man bellowed, pointing to me with his sword.

They rushed forward. Freya's sword lay near my feet. I released the woman and snatched up the weapon. As I faced the Jotuns, I glimpsed Freya staring in wonder from me to the charging barbarians. I heard their captain shouting orders.

"Strike them both down. Be sure the man does not escape!"

They came at me in a bunch. The light, straight sword in my hand flashed out viciously. I was a fair hand with a saber, for it was a sport I had practiced in university days. Except for its straightness, this sword was like the blades I had used.

It bit through a Jotun throat, then swung in a slicing slash at his nearest comrade's neck. Both men crumpled, but the others came on. I knew I was done for. Real life isn't like the movies. One man just can't stand off six in a sword fight.

"We are at the edge of the cliff," Freya said calmly. "Another step backward and we fall."

"Take care not to push the man over the cliff," shouted the Jotun captain apprehensively. "We must not lose his body!"

Whatever its reason, their caution gave me a chance I would not have had otherwise. I stood up against their stabbing blades, fending off savage thrusts. But such a battle could not go on for long. Already my arm was tiring, and I was exhausted by all I had gone through.

"He weakens!" roared the Jotun captain. "Thrust home!"

At that moment I heard a thunder of approaching hoofs.

"Help comes!" Freya cried. "My kinsman and the Jarl Thor!"

The Jotun warriors stopped and swung around. A bellow of rage and terror went up from them. Two riders were charging toward us, from Asgard, followed by a hurrying troop. One was a helmeted, gold-haired man, whose handsome face was wild with anger. The other's red face and small eyes were blazing. His yellow beard bristling, he swung a huge hammer that to me seemed his only weapon.

"The Hammerer!" cried the Jotuns.

They bolted in frantic fear toward their horses. But they were too late. A terrible bull-roar of rage came from the bearded, bareheaded giant. His huge hammer smashed a Jotun's helmet and skull like cardboard. Without slackening his horse's stride, the gigantic Hammerer swung his awful weapon at another Jotun's head.

"It's the Jarl Thor and my kinsman Frey!" Freya stated coolly.

Thor, mightiest of the old gods of legend, strongest of Aesir? Frey, the mythical kinsman of Freya? I shrugged in defeated skepticism.

None of the fleeing Jotuns reached their horses. The lightninglike sword of Frey stabbed two as they ran, and the terrible hammer of bearded Thor smashed down the others. Then Thor and Frey wheeled their horses. The Hammerer uttered another roar of rage and spurred straight at me.

"Here's a Jotun dog we missed!"

Before I could move, his great hammer, bright-red with new blood, was already raised. I swayed drunkenly, exhausted, unable to defend myself from that terrible weapon.

"Wait!" Freya cried.

The hammer was checked in mid-air. No ordinary man could have halted its downward rush so effortlessly.

"Is he not one of the Jotun skrellings who attacked you?" rumbled Thor.

"He cannot be," Freya said. "For they tried even harder to kill him than me, and he fought valiantly against them."

Frey hurriedly dismounted. His handsome face was drawn with worry as he ran to the woman and caught her shoulders.

"You're not harmed, Freya?" he asked anxiously.

"No, by the help of this outlander," she said. "Jarl Keith is his name, and he says he came from beyond Niffleheim."

"It's true," I panted. "I came in that flying ship."

I pointed to the beach far below, where my rocket plane rested between boulders. They stared down at it.

"So you outlanders can build flying ships," Frey said wonderingly. "Your civilization must be far different from ours. Odin will wish to question this outlander. We'll take him to Asgard with us."

Odin, chief of the old Norse gods, king of the mythical Aesir? I shook my head and gave up the fight against disbelief.

"Very well," growled Thor reluctantly. "I still think he looks like a Jotun."

Frey brought me the horse of a dead Jotun. By now, the troop that had hurried after Frey and Thor reached us. They were all big, fair-haired men, armored in mail brynjas and helmets, obviously disappointed at missing the fight.

I mounted, unable to lose the dreamlike quality of the experiences. With the troop of horsemen following. I rode beside Freya, Thor and Frey. I heard the clatter of hoofs, the rumble of voices, felt the saddle beneath me, and the motion of the horse. But nothing seemed real. My body grasped the actuality, yet my tired, harried brain refused to accept it. My eyes were so puzzled and shot with blood that Freya looked at me sympathetically.

"You can rest in Asgard. Jarl Keith." she said. "And you have nothing to fear from my people."

"I do not fear," I answered thickly, "but my dazed mind makes me unhappy. Are you people really the old gods?"

"Gods," she repeated. "I do not understand you, Jarl Keith. There are no gods except the three Norns and their mother, Wyrd, the fates whom we worship."

I clenched my teeth and stared straight ahead. If they weren't the ancient Norse gods, why did they give themselves, their city, the lands around them, the names I had found in the legends? On the other hand, it couldn't be a fake, for they seemed genuinely bewildered by me and my questions. Naturally they might have been fairly recent immigrants to this weird blind spot, perhaps the tenth or fifteenth generation. In that case, they wouldn't be immortals, of course, and there would be a perfectly reasonable explanation for their names and those of their city and surroundings. But would recent colonists dare the vengeance of their gods by taking their names? I had to change that question when another thought struck me. Even if the colony were thousands of years old, there would still be some remembrance of the Aesir — the old gods! But these people worshiped the Norns and their mother, Wyrd, which meant they were not gods and did not regard the Aesir as supernatural beings!

Defeatedly I stopped thinking when we reached the rainbow bridge. Five hundred feet long, it consisted of brilliantly painted slabs of stone, laid across two huge arched beams of massive, silvery metal. Far beneath this giddy span, the green sea rolled between the promontory and the island, Asgard. My hair stood up in fright as we rode our horses up the arch. Their hoofs clattered on the stone, proving the solidity of the bridge. But I shrank from looking over either side, for there were no railings or low walls. But neither the Aesir nor their horses showed apprehension.

Bifrost Bridge hung in the sky like a rainbow frozen into stone. And I, Keith Masters, with Thor, Frey and Freya of the old Aesir, was riding across it into Asgard, the mythical city of the gods!

CHAPTER IV

Odin Speaks

THE BRIDGE ended in a massive guard-house of gray stone, built sheer on the precipitous edge of Asgard. The only entrance to the city beyond was by an arched way through the fort, which was, barred by metal gates. But as our horses clattered over the stupendous bridge, a guard blew a long, throbbing call on a great horn that hung in a sling.

Our horses paused. Warily I glanced down into the abyss and looked at the island more closely. I noted that in the eastern cliffs was a deep fiord with a narrow entrance, in which floated several dozen ships. Dragon-ships like those of the old Vikings, they were forty to eighty feet long, with brazen beaks on their bows and sails furled and oars stacked. From the fiord, a steep path led upward to the plateau.

In answer to the blast on the horn, a tall, lordly man in gleaming mail and helmet came out on the tower above.

"Open wide your gates, Heimdall!" boomed Thor impatiently. "Are we to be kept waiting here till we rot?"

"Softly, Thor," Frey said to the Hammerer. "It was Heimdall, remember, whose keen eyes saw Freya and the Jotuns and warned us."

Heimdall, the warder of the guardhouse, waved his hand to us. Winches groaned, and the barred gates swung inward. We spurred forward. I was glad to leave that unrailed bridge over the abyss. We rode right through the arched tunnel that pierced the guardhouse, and clattered onto a stone-paved plaza.

Asgard lay before me.

Involuntarily I slacked my bridle and stared at the great gray castles that were built in a ring around the sheer edge of the lofty island. All twenty had been built of gray stone hewn from the rock of the island itself, and all were tiled with thin stone slates. Each consisted of a big, rectangular, two-storied hall, with two branching lower wings and two guard-towers. They faced toward a far huger pile that rose from the center of the island.

The largest castle had four guard-towers, and its vast, stone-tiled roof loomed over the rest of Asgard like a man-made mountain. Between this great hall and the ring of smaller castles lay small fields and cobbled streets of stone houses and workshops.

Hundreds of the people of Asgard were in the streets and fields.

All were fair-haired, blue-eyed and large-statured. Many of the men wore helmets and mailed brynjas, and were armed with sword, ax or bow. Other men wore metal rings around their necks, but they went about their tasks cheerfully enough. The women wore long blue or white gowns, with wimpled hoods. There were scarcely any children.

"Must be an unbelievably low birthrate here," I muttered. "That could be due to the hard radiation effect."

The faint, eldritch green glow pervaded this island, like the mainland. It was certainly exhilarating. It was restoring my vigor with amazing speed. But if it was actually gamma or a similar hard radiation, as I suspected, it would be bound to cause a partial sterility among people who were continually exposed to it.

We spurred toward the central castle, halted our horses on a stone plaza guarded by a file of soldiery.

"This is Valhalla, the castle of our king," Freya told me as we dismounted. "Courage, Jarl Keith. Odin will explain all to you."

The touch of her slim white fingers seemed to steady me. Valhalla, the legendary gathering hall of the gods, had stunned me. I grinned weakly and followed Thor as he clanked through the arched entrance and strode down a stone corridor into a vast hall.

The place was two hundred feet wide and six hundred feet long! Ninety feet above us were the great beams that supported the enormous gabled roof. Narrow, slit-like windows admitted too little light to dispel the shadows, but I could see that the walls were hung with brilliant tapestries. The stone floor held massive tables and benches.

In the center was a great sunken hearth, where a few dying brands still smoldered. Facing this, on a raised stone dais against the south wall, sat Odin, king of the Aesir. He was wrapped in a blue-gray mantle, and wore a gleaming eagle-helmet. Thor led our little group across the shadowy hall and raised his hammer in salute.

"Hail, king and father! The Jotuns dared to attack the lady Freya. Frey and I killed the skrellings, and have brought this man. He looks like a Jotun to me, but he claims he is an outlander."

Freya stepped forward, her slim figure martial in her gleaming white mail, her beautiful white face wrathful.

"Thor is stupid as ever, lord Odin! Anyone can see this man is an outlander from beyond Niffleheim."

"Let the man speak for himself," Odin said in a heavy, rolling voice.

The king of the Aesir seemed to be a powerful, vigorous man of about fifty years of age. His short beard was gray. His left eye was missing, destroyed by the accident or battle that had also left a white scar on his face. But he radiated such deep, stern power and wisdom that I felt like a child before him.

"You say you came from beyond Niffleheim?" he asked.

"Yes, lord Odin," I answered unsteadily. "I was traveling over that icy waste in my flying ship. A storm caught me and flung me far north, toward this strange land which I could not even see until I was hurled into it."

"So the outland peoples have been learning science?" Odin asked thoughtfully. "It must be so, if they can build flying craft."

"Yes, and I am one of the scientists of my people," I said. "Yet I cannot understand this strange land. It cannot be seen from outside. It is warm compared with the polar cold outside, and it seems flooded with some mysterious force."

"If you cannot understand these things," Odin rumbled, "then the science of your outland peoples cannot be deep as our ancient one."

I was more stunned than ever. The Aesir seemed utterly without modern scientific tools, weapons and instruments, yet their ruler was calmly deprecating the science of the modern world.

"I cannot understand you, lord Odin!" I burst out. "Asgard, all the Aesir, and the Jotuns have been deemed but legend for many centuries. Yet in this hidden land I find you have the names of the old gods, and have called your city Asgard. Most of all, I do not understand why you speak of the science of my race as though you knew a much deeper science. I have seen no evidences of scientific knowledge in this land at all!"

"Outlander, who call yourself Jarl Keith," Odin replied, "we Aesir are men, not gods. But we have lived for many centuries in Asgard, and many legends may have risen about us in the outer world."

"You've lived here for centuries?" I gasped incredulously. "Do you mean that you are immortal?"

"Not immortal. We can be killed by war, accident or starvation. But we do not grow old, and neither do we sicken or die of disease. We do possess an ancient science, deeper and different than your outland science.

"But because it once brought us disaster, we prefer not to encourage research in it, nor use it in our everyday lives. We Aesir were the first civilized race of Earth. For we grew to civilization in the place where life itself first evolved — beneath the crust of Earth."

"Inside Earth?" I exclaimed unbelievingly. "Why, not one of our biologists would agree!"

"Yet it is so," said Odin broodingly. "There are great spaces beneath the crust of the planet, mighty hollows formed by its unequal cooling. It was in one of those spaces beneath this northern part of the globe that life first began. For in those hollows are great masses of imbedded radioactive elements.

"Their radiation, powerfully drenching certain compounds of carbon, hydrogen, phosphorus, sulfur and other elements, which erosion carried down into the subterranean spaces, transformed those unstable compounds into new, complex chemical compounds. They never could have formed on the surface. Those organic compounds finally formed into cells capable of assimilation and reproduction.

"A rapid evolution of those first subterranean living cells into more complex creatures took place. It was rapid because the penetrating radiation in that subterranean space affected the genes of all living things and caused a proliferation of mutants, a constant flood of new forms. Thus, the first living things, the first plants and insects and animals, were born beneath Earth's crust.

"From there, they spread out onto Earth's surface, and soon multiplied vastly. But evolution was more rapid in the subterranean spaces. For the gene-affecting radiation was more powerful there than on the surface. Thus more mutants evolved there. So it was in the subterranean spaces that the first mammals and the first men evolved. Many of those men found their way out to the surface.

"They spread over Earth as wandering, half-animal savages who slowly developed through the ages. But the human beings who remained in the sheltered subterranean world developed far more swiftly. Those people had become intelligent when the men of the surface were still brutes. Those people in the underworld developed a great civilization and deep knowledge of science. They were my people, the Aesir.

"Generations of us lived and died in the great, hollow underground world we called Muspelheim. But then our scientific progress brought catastrophe. One of our scientists, ignoring my warnings, believed that he could enable us to live indefinitely without aging or sickening.

"His theory was that by accelerating the natural disintegration of the radioactive substances in our subterranean world, they would emit a terrific flood of radiation. It would destroy all disease bacteria and deliver us from sickness. It also would constantly renew the cells in our bodies by stimulating their unceasing regeneration."

Odin paused, and a shudder seemed to run through all the Aesir in that great hall, Valhalla.

"Against my orders, he carried out the experiment that brought catastrophe to Muspelheim. The process got beyond his control. All the radioactive matter in our subterranean world blazed up. We Aesir fled up from our underworld to the our subterranean world blazed up. We Aesir fled up from our underworld to the surface. We found that the mainland yonder, which we called Midgard, was populated by two of the barbarous races of the upper Earth.

"One of those races, whom we called the Jotuns because of their great stature, were quite numerous. A people of savage, brutal warriors, lacking all learning, they dwelt in the dark city Jotunheim, which lies on the southern shore of the mainland Midgard. The other race we called the Alfings, for they were stunted men who dwelt mostly in the small caves under Midgard, through fear of the Jotuns.

"The Jotuns at first pretended friendliness toward us, and learned our language. We had taken this island of Asgard for our home, and had built our castles here, and connected it to the mainland by the bridge Bifrost, whose beams the Alfings forged for us. Then the Jotuns suddenly unmasked their hatred and attacked us here in Asgard.

"Almost they overcame us, for to surprise was added treachery. But by calling upon our scientific powers, we repelled the Jotuns. Aghast at the dreadful forces our science loosed upon them, they gladly ceased attacking us. Yet they have always hated us, and we have lived in a hostile armed truce with them for twenty centuries.

"Yes, for two thousand years have I and most of my people lived here in Asgard. The terrific blaze of radioactive fire which our rash scientist kindled in Muspelheim far below drenches all this land with penetrating radiation. Even as he had hoped, it kills all disease bacteria and rejuvenates our tissues. We do not sicken or age, and can live indefinitely, unless killed in war or accident. But because the radiation has a strong sterilizing effect, our number has never increased.

"The Jotuns and Alfings, who dwell in the mainland Midgard, are also kept unaging by the radiation. And it refracts all light around this land. It also causes the northern lights that stream from this place into the skies. Here in Asgard we have lived thus for all these centuries. Though we chiefs of the Aesir retain the deep scientific knowledge we developed long ago in Muspelheim, we have chosen not to delve deeper.

"It was such delving that brought disaster to our subterranean home. We want no more such disasters! We are content to live here in simple fashion, without depending too utterly on science. We know from bitter experience that science can be perverted to catastrophic results by reckless and unscrupulous men."

His heavy voice ceased. I stood staring at him, my mind dizzy. Incredible as it seemed, his story was scientifically sound. It explained nearly all the enigmas I had met in this mystery land.

"You have lived here for centuries," I mused. "Dim rumors of your powers, your city Asgard, and your war with the Jotuns, must have reached the outer world. These rumors became myths that made you gods."

"It must be so," Odin agreed. "Long ago, a party of the Aesir went beyond the ice on an important mission. Some of them did not return. Now I believe those lost ones reached the outer world. They probably died soon, from lack of the rejuvenating radiation. But their stories of us may have begun those myths."

"So I am thought a mythical god in the outer world, eh?" Thor guffawed.

"It is true," I said earnestly. "And also lord Odin, and Frey and Freya. But there's one thing I can't understand. Those Jotuns who attacked me and Freya seemed intent on killing or capturing me. It was as though they expected me, and were waiting to seize me. Yet how could they possibly know I was coming?"

Odin frowned. "I do not know, but I do not like it. It may be that the Jotuns —"

His voice trailed off, and he stared abstractedly beyond me. Somehow the tone of his voice had chilled me.

"But enough of that now," he said abruptly. "We shall talk later of these things and of the outer world from whence you come. Now Jarl Keith is to be an honored guest of the Aesir."

"I can't claim that title," I replied. "I am no chieftain in my own land. I'm only a scientist."

"Any man who dared Niffleheim's ice has won the title of jarl," he declared. "You shall rest in this castle. And tonight, Jarl Keith, you sit with the Aesir at our nightly feast, here in Valhalla."

CHAPTER V

Shadow of Loki

SLOWLY I awoke to the realization that a hand was gently shaking my shoulder. I saw at once that it was twilight. I had slept exhaustedly for several hours in this spacious, stone-walled room. I lay on a wooden bed whose posts were carved into wolf's heads. There were two heavy chairs with hide seats, and a big chest covered by a brilliant tapestry. Broad open windows looked out across the twilit city of Asgard.

The hand shaking my shoulder was that of a thrall. The servant, a grizzled, middle-aged man, wore the metal ring of servitude around his neck.

"The feast in Valhalla begins soon, lord," he said as I sat up. "I have brought you proper raiment."

He pointed to a helmet and garments such as the Aesir wore, which he had placed on the chest.

"All right, if I'm supposed to dress in the fashion," I said dubiously.

As he bowed and left, I went to the window. The rapidly darkening sky had partly cleared of storm clouds. In the southwest, a bloody, murky sunset glowed evilly crimson. The shaggy hills and ridges of Midgard stood out black against it.

Somewhere on the mainland, miles away at its southern end, was the dark city of Jotunheim. Somewhere in the caves of that rocky land dwelt the dwarfed Alfings. And far below all this land, if Odin had told the truth, lay the great subterranean world of Muspelheim. There blazed the terrific atomic radiation that made this a warm country where no man could sicken or grow old enough to die.

Beneath me, as dusk fell over Asgard, I could see a cheerful bustle of activity. Armed soldiers, who had been training with sword and buckler on a nearby field, were now trooping through the twilight toward Valhalla. Smoke was rising from great castles and humble stone houses. I glimpsed hunters riding over Bifrost Bridge, the carcasses of small deer slung over their saddles. As Asgard's gates were opened, I heard the throbbing call of the warder's great horn welcoming them.

Was it possible that I was actually here in the mythical city of the gods? It certainly was hard to believe. But even more incredible was Odin's saga. If he and the other Aesir chiefs possessed such profound scientific knowledge, why did they and all their people live so primitively?

"I suppose it's true," I muttered. "They don't age or grow sick, so they can live pleasantly enough without using science. Anyhow, they had a damned unpleasant experience with one reckless scientist. It's no wonder they don't encourage research." Slowly I shook my head. "No. I'll wake up and find it's just a dream. But I'd hate to have it disappear before I could see Freya again. Wonder if she'll be at the feast."

That thought spurred me into taking off my heavy coat, breeches and boots. The helmet, woolen trunks, mail coat, buskins, belt and long sword and dagger looked uncomfortably like stage props. But women are funny about unfamiliar clothing. Just think how they laugh when the telenews shows them styles they wore a couple of decades ago! I didn't want Freya to have that reaction to me.

But when I took off my own shirt to don the Aesir garments, my hand touched something that hung from my neck. It was the rune key! I had completely forgotten it since entering the blind spot. Now, however, I suddenly thought of the rune rhyme.

> *Rune key am I,*
> *Chaining dark evil,*
> *Midgard snake, Fenris,*
> *And Loki, arch-devil.*

Why, I wondered, had I heard no mention of Loki? Everything else in the old Norse myths seemed to have some solid basis here, but I had heard nothing of the traitor Aesir. I decided to ask Odin about that at my first opportunity, as I tucked the gold cylinder inside my new shirt and laced up the mail brynja over it.

Hardly had I done so when the grizzled thrall again appeared at the door of my chamber.

"King Odin summons you to the feast, lord."

I quickly put on the heavy, gleaming helmet. Feeling stiff as a ham actor in the strange costume, I followed the thrall down stone stairs to the great hall. The thrall shouted a loud announcement.

"The Jarl Keith, from the outlands beyond Niffleheim!"

The voices and laughter died down, and every eye turned toward me with eager curiosity. Valhalla blazed with light from torches set in the walls and the great fire blazing high in the central hearth. The scores of tables now bore metal and earthenware dishes loaded with food. Tall flagons and drinking horns were replenished by swift serving-maidens.

At these tables sat the chief captains and warriors of the Aesir. Hundreds of big, fair-haired men, helmets laid aside, their mail glistening in the torchlight, were feasting and drinking. At the table raised upon the dais by the southern wall sat the nobles of the Aesir and their ladies. In his high, carved chair in the middle sat Odin. Beside him was a woman of matronly beauty, his queen, the lady Frigga.

"Jarls and captains of the Aesir," Odin boomed. "Drink welcome to the Jarl Keith, our guest and friend from beyond Niffleheim."

"Skoal to the Jarl Keith!" roared bearded Thor, winking jovially at me as he raised his huge drinking-horn.

"Skoal!" pealed Freya's silver voice. Every voice in Valhalla hall repeated the greeting. Hundreds of drinking-horns were raised. Odin waved me toward a seat at his table of nobles, between Freya and the delicately lovely wife of Thor. As I took the chair, serving-maids brought me a great slab of beef on a platter, and a horn of mead. I tasted the drink curiously. It was thin, sweet and potent.

Freya leaned toward me. She was dressed now like the other Aesir ladies, in a long white linen gown. Her bright hair was bound by a silver circlet, her dress belted by a heavy metal girdle studded with flashing emeralds.

"Shall I name the others for you, Jarl Keith? You will meet them all soon."

At my right, beyond giant Thor and his wife, sat three other sons of Odin — Vidar, Vali and Hermod, tall and fair-haired, stalwart men all. There was Heimdall, the warder of Asgard gate, whom I had already seen. Niord was a squat, jovial bald man of middle age, with his wife Skadi. Forseti was a sober young man, apparently much respected by the other Aesir.

To my left, beyond Freya, sat Frey and his lovely wife, Gerda. Beyond them were Bragi, a gentle-looking man with dreaming eyes, his wife, the noble-featured Idun; Aegir, a gaunt, white-bearded old sea-king, and his aged wife, Ran. At the- table-end sat Tyr, a young man but most gloomy and silent of any in the hall. Drinking moodily, he watched the merry feasters with brooding eyes.

"Tyr is always dark and silent," Freya explained, "but not in battle. He is a berserk."

I remembered the legend of the berserks — men who went blood-mad in battle, and fought with unhuman frenzy, without mail.

"How is it that some of you are old, if the radiation keeps you all from aging?" I asked.

"They were old when the catastrophe first kindled the radiation below. Since then, none of them has grown older. The few children born here grow normally till they reach maturity, and then do not age further."

"You've all lived here in Asgard for centuries on centuries," I muttered. "It seems repulsive."

"Not all of us, Jarl Keith," said Freya. "I am not centuries old!"

She smiled when I looked at her doubtfully.

"Your name was known and worshiped in the outer world centuries ago, Freya."

"My mother's mother was named Freya also," she explained. "She was sister to Frey, who sits beside you. She and her husband Odur were among the party of Aesir Odin mentioned, who perished in a mission beyond Niffleheim. But Freya left two daughters, Hnoss and Gersemi. Gersemi was my own mother. She perished from drowning twenty years ago, soon after I was born."

"Then you're really only twenty years old?" I exclaimed. "I'm glad of that!"

"Why should you be glad, Jarl Keith?" she asked quite innocently.

I was spared a reply by an interruption to the feast. Tall Heimdall stood up and called:

"A saga from the king of skalds, Bragi!"

When the feasters took up the cry, Bragi rose. Smiling, he went to a great harp at the end of the hall. His fingers touched the strings, and rippling, shivering music welled out. He sang in a clear, strong voice:

> *Give ear, all ye Aesir, Sons of the morning,*
> *Wise men and warriors,*
> *Men with great hearts!*
> *Ye who fared upward,*
> *From Muspelheim's fire-hell,*
> *Daring all terrors*
> *To seek a new land!*

Bragi sang on, describing the migration of the Aesir from their disaster-smitten underworld, their repulse of the Jotuns, the hunt and the battle of their ships along Midgard's coast, and the fury of the sea.

"Skoal, Bragi!" roared the audience, and all raised their horns.

I drank with the others. The potent mead made me a little dizzy.

I nearly forgot I was Keith Masters. I was the Jarl Keith, sitting beside Freya in Valhalla, feasting and shouting.

"Now for the games," Odin announced.

A gleeful yell came from the warriors.

"What games are these?" I asked.

"Sword-play with blunted blades, and wrestling," Freya said. "As a guest, Jarl Keith, you'll take part in them, of course."

I saw everyone looking expectantly at me. Somewhat sobered, I stood up.

"I'm but a fair swordsman, lord Odin," I said, "yet I'll join in."

"Who will try sword-play with the outland Jarl?" Odin asked. "Tyr, you are our best swordsman."

"No, lord Odin, not I," the berserk Tyr answered broodingly. "You know that a sword in my hand brings the madness on me."

"I'll face Jarl Keith," said Frey, standing up and smiling at me.

We walked around to the open space in front of the tables. There we were given gauntlets, shields, and two long swords whose points had been cut off.

"Who delivers three stout blows on his opponent's helmet wins the game," Odin stated.

The game appeared dangerous to me, for our faces were quite unprotected. I hadn't much hope of besting Frey; but I was determined not to show any semblance of fear before Freya and these fierce warriors.

Frey's blade clashed against mine. Next instant, I realized I could never meet his equal. Centuries of practice had made him unhumanly skillful. His blade flew like a streak of light and crashed on my helmet. As I staggered from the stunning blow, he hit my helmet again. A roar went up from the crowd. Resentment gripped me, and I lashed out savagely at Frey's head.

By sheer luck, the unexpected stroke caught his mailed shoulder. When he stumbled, I smote down on his helmet.

"Well done, Jarl Keith!" roared the bull voice of Thor.

But Frey recovered before I did. His blade became a blur of steel in front of me. Grimly I tried to hold him off. But he soon got in his third blow.

"Are you hurt, Jarl Keith?" asked Frey solicitously.

"Only my pride," I said ruefully, as I put down the sword and shield.

Thor strode around the table to me. His bearded red face and little eyes were twinkling with jovial expectation.

"You look like a wrestler, Jarl from the outlands," he boomed. "Will you try a fall with me?"

"Aye, a match between Thor and the outland Jarl!" the audience shouted.

"Jarl Keith hasn't rested!" Freya cried indignantly to the Hammerer. "It's not fair!"

"I'm ready," I said coolly to Thor. I realized to the full that the chances of my overcoming the giant were infinitesimal. But I realized, too, that all this was a kind of hazing which these Vikings gave to any newcomer. Thor tossed aside his hammer. We faced each other, hands extended, seeking a grip.

I was a fair wrestler, and I knew that my only chance was to overcome Thor by a quick trick that he might not know.

As the giant grabbed for me, I slipped past him. Leaping to his back, I got a half-nelson on him before he could expect it.

A mighty shout went up from the watchers as they saw the Hammerer claw furiously to pull me loose. Furiously I hung on.

With one sturdy arm against the back of his heavily cabled neck, and my legs braced, I strained to force his huge head downward. For a moment I thought I had a chance to win the match. Then a bull-roar of rage came from Thor.

He jerked his head upward with such tremendous force that my hold was torn loose.

Like an enraged bear, the Hammerer whirled and caught me around the waist.

This was wrestling in his style, all strength and little science. His huge arms crushed me, though I exerted all my strength to win free. I felt the lacings of my mail coat burst under the pressure as I strained frantically to break his hold. But he picked me up like a child and slammed me down upon the stone floor.

"Well done," he roared as he let me go. "You almost conquered me with your outland tricks, Jarl Keith. You will have to teach them to me."

"Some other time," I gasped, panting for breath as I stumbled to my feet. I turned toward the king. "If you are satisfied, lord Odin, I'll take part in no more games now."

Odin smiled. "You have borne yourself well, Jarl Keith, and —"

His voice ceased as his stern face seemed to freeze.

When I saw that he was staring at my chest, I looked down. The bursting mail coat had let the rune key dangle in full view.

"The rune key!" he whispered.

Everyone in great Valhalla was speechless, staring in horror at the ancient gold cylinder that hung outside my coat.

"The rune key!" Odin repeated hoarsely. "It has come back to Asgard. This is the day for which dark Loki has waited!"

CHAPTER VI

Ancient Science

THE FROZEN stillness in Valhalla was appalling. Aesir nobles and warriors all seemed turned to stone as they stared at the golden cylinder hanging from my neck. I could hear the torches guttering, the snap of logs on the blazing hearth, and the dull moan of the sea wind around Valhalla's lofty eaves. It was as though the feast of the Aesir had been smitten by chill terror.

"Where did you get that key, Jarl Keith?" Odin asked me hoarsely.

"Why, my comrades fished it out of the sea beyond the icepack — beyond Niffleheim," I answered bewilderedly.

A deep groan went up from the entire gathering. I turned to them unhappily, feeling like a hunted animal that knows it has done no wrong, yet still is persecuted.

"Why did you bring it into this land?" Odin demanded fiercely.

"I don't know," I blurted. Remembering the queer alien hunch that had made me find the key, I added: "Some strange whim in my mind told me where it was and warned me not to throw it away."

"Loki's work!" Odin whispered. "The evil one has cast forces abroad that have brought back the rune key that will set him free."

Thor's face flamed crimson as he sprang to his feet, clutching his mighty weapon.

"The arch-traitor still seeks to ruin Asgard and the Aesir!" he roared in overpowering rage. "Oh, that I could bring Miolnir down upon his skull this moment!"

"Even your strength and mighty weapon would fail against the dark science of Loki," Odin said somberly.

I looked down bewilderedly at the gold cylinder hanging on my chest. Into my mind flashed the last lines of the rune-rhyme graven on it.

> *While I lie far,*
> *The Aesir safe are.*
> *Bring me not home*
> *Lest Ragnarok come.*

Those lines seemed to throb in my mind like a beating drum of black, dire menace that cannot be seen yet can be felt.

"I do not understand, lord Odin," I faltered. "Have I done wrong in bringing this small and apparently harmless key into your land?"

"Because you brought it," Odin stated, calm at last, "we are threatened with doom. A terrible menace has been a shadow over us for all these long centuries. That is the key which alone can loose the evil traitor Loki, who long has been prisoned."

When he saw me pale at his words, his deep, heavy voice rumbled comfortingly through the frozen silence.

"It is not your fault, Jarl Keith. I see it all now. It was Loki's power that brought you and the rune key here. Yes, from the gloomy prison where his body lies helpless, Loki's mind reached forth through his deep craft of scientific powers. He caused you to fish that rune key from the sea, and raised the storm that blew you hither. Aye, and it was to take from you the key that would free their dark lord that the Jotuns attacked you when you arrived."

"But who is Loki?" I asked bewilderedly. "In the old myths of the northland, there was a tale of a traitor by that name, who sought to destroy you —"

"Aye, a black traitor was accursed Loki!" shouted Thor. "The shame and the curse of the Aesir, since first he was born."

"Aye, traitor he was, indeed," said Odin somberly. "Yet long ago, when we dwelt in the underworld of Muspelheim, Loki was the most honored of the Aesir, next to myself. Handsome, valiant, cunning, and learned, he was second only to me among the Aesir. But Loki, the greatest scientist of my people, longed for power. His experiments endangered us all, time and again. Finally, against my orders, Loki brought catastrophe on our great and lovely underworld."

"Then Loki was the scientist you told me of!" I exclaimed. "He kindled the atomic fires of Muspelheim and nearly destroyed you!"

Odin nodded. "Loki was that rash scientist of whom I spoke. Seeking to kindle a radiation that would keep us ever young, he touched off atomic fires that engulfed Muspelheim and forced us to flee to this upper world. I should have punished Loki then for his reckless disobedience. But I did not, because the flood of radiation would keep us almost immortal in this land. Instead I warned him that nobody must tamper further with the raving atomic fires below.

"Loki agreed to tamper no more with those awful forces. But his promise was worth nothing. Secretly, here in Asgard, he traveled back into fiery Muspelheim, and began experimenting again. He hoped to forge such tremendous weapons from those forces that he could displace me as ruler of the Aesir and conquer all Earth. My son Baldur discovered Loki's forbidden researches in deep Muspelheim. To prevent Baldur from exposing him, Loki slew him. But he had already exposed himself.

"Loki fled from Asgard. Taking with him his two hideous pets, the wolf Fenris and the Midgard snake, he fled to dark Jotunheim. There he allied himself with the brutal Jotuns. He knew they hated the Aesir, so he incited them to attack us, promising that with his scientific powers, he would help them conquer and sack Asgard.

"That was the time of which I told you, Jarl Keith, when surprise and treachery almost enabled the Jotuns to conquer us. The Jotuns, led by Loki and aided by the hellish forces his science devised, would have overcome us had I not used my own scientific powers to defeat Loki's and had we not all fought valiantly. We repelled the Jotuns with great slaughter."

Thor grinned and nodded, but his giant face reddened with hatred as Odin continued.

"Defeated, Loki fled with his wolf and serpent into the labyrinth of caves in Midgard. We followed him to the cave in which he hid, but Loki, in his extremity, bargained cunningly for his life. Loki called out to us: 'I have an instrument which can destroy all Asgard and the Aesir, by loosing the sea upon the atomic fires of Muspelheim. Unless you agree to spare my life, I will use that secret and you will all perish with me.'"

"'We agree then to spare your life, Loki,' I answered. 'You have our pledge, if you surrender that deadly instrument.' Loki surrendered the instrument to me. And then I told him: 'We agreed to spare your life, Loki — but that is all! Though you shall remain alive, you will no longer be a menace to us, for we shall prison you eternally in this cave to which you fled.'

"And we did that to Loki, Jarl Keith. We cast him into a state of suspended animation by filling his cave with a gas whose scientific secret I had discovered. That gas paralyzed the functions of the body by freezing, but left the mind conscious as ever. Into that waking, frozen sleep we cast Loki and his two hideous pets. Then we closed that cave forever with a door that was not of metal or stone, but of invulnerable force.

"That wall of energy was a screen of vibrations controlled by the generator inside a tiny projector. You, Jarl Keith, have that projector — the rune key! Only the rune key can unlock the door of Loki's cave-prison. Until it is unlocked, Loki must lie there with his two dreadful familiars in suspended animation.

"But though Loki's body lies frozen, his mind is awake and

active, and he seeks by mental forces to free himself. We had given the wardership of the rune key to Odur, husband of Freya, one of our greatest jarls. Loki's mind worked from afar upon Odur by telepathic command, attempting to force the keeper of the key to release Loki.

"Fearing that Loki's telepathic orders might some day succeed, I commanded Odur to take the rune key and travel to the great ocean far outside icy Niffleheim, and fling it into the deepest sea. Then, I thought, Loki would not be able to bring the key back into Asgard, and would never manage to escape his doom. Odur took the rune key and went beyond the ice of Niffleheim, and flung the key into the ocean as I bade.

"But before he could return across the ice, Odur and his wife Freya and their party were lost. I think now that they reached the lands of your outer world, and that their tales of the Aesir and Asgard started the myths you mentioned, Jarl Keith. But we thought ourselves safe, with the rune key resting in the ocean deeps far outside Asgard.

"For even did a stranger chance to find the key in some future day, the runes upon it would warn him. In case he could not read the runes, the key was constructed to telepath a constant thought message. He would receive a constant mental warning to get rid of the key."

"So that's why I felt that sensation of ominous warning, after I first touched the key!" I muttered.

"That is why," Odin replied gravely; "And yet you, Jarl Keith, were influenced by the even stronger commands of Loki. You kept the key, and brought it back into Asgard. And now Loki, through his allies, the Jotuns, will seek to get the rune key from us, to use it to free himself. And if Loki is ever freed again, he will lead the hosts of Jotunheim once more against Asgard. And it might well be that Asgard falls, that the Aesir perish!"

I listened in horror. Not for a moment did I doubt Odin was telling the truth. The ancient science of these Aesir, though neglecting mechanical discoveries for which they had little need, had clearly surpassed us in the study of the subtlest forces of the Universe.

Yes, I knew now what the two contending, alien voices in my mind had been. The constant telepathic warning of the rune key projector itself — and the more powerful mental command of dreaded Loki!

"I did not know, lord Odin," I declared with sincere regret. "Had I dreamed that the rune key was what it really is, I'd never have brought it here."

"You had no way of knowing, Jarl Keith," he answered. "And the attempt of Loki has failed. The Jotuns he sent to take the key failed in their task, and we still hold it."

I took the little gold cylinder from around my neck and handed it to him. The instant I parted with it, I felt relieved of that throbbing, warning sensation which had incessantly oppressed me. Odin took the key. While all in Valhalla watched, he solemnly handed it to the wide-eyed Freya.

"Your grandfather was keeper of the key, Freya, and the office descends to you," the Aesir king stated. "You shall hold it until we take council and decide what to do with it."

"Couldn't you just destroy the thing?" I asked.

Odin shook his head. "You know little of our science, outland Jarl. The projector in the rune key maintains the energy screen that bars Loki's cave-prison. Destroying the key would destroy that screen. Let no fear enter your hearts, men of the Aesir. Loki is still prisoned, and shall remain so. Not yet has the hour come when the evil one shall escape."

A fierce roar of shouts crashed from the throng, as their swords and axes flashed high in the torchlight.

"Our swords for Asgard!"

"It is well," Odin said with somber pride. "Now let this feast of ill omen end. Heimdall, keep closest watch on Asgard's gates to-night. Loki's mind knows the key is here, and he might telepathically incite the Jotuns to attack us and secure it. And you, Frey, see that your castle is well guarded, to protect your kinswoman and the key."

Freya stood fingering the cord of the rune key. She looked at me with wordless, troubled appeal as she left. I followed her into the night.

The eldritch faint green glow of the streaming, tingling radiation clung to the towering castles. No aurora was visible, for that streamed up outside the blind spot. A haggard Moon was shining through flying storm clouds. The driving north wind wailed keen and cold. From far below came the dim, distant booming of the surf as the stormy ocean dashed against the cliffs. Freya turned toward me, her eyes dark and big.

"Jarl Keith, I am afraid!" she whispered. "I, who never knew fear before, am fearful now. If Loki is loosed —"

"There's no chance of that, while you and your people hold the key," I encouraged her. "And even if he were set free, he is only one man."

"He is evil itself." She shuddered. "I never saw Loki. Long centuries before my birth, he was prisoned. But I have heard the tales of the other Aesir. I know that, in their secret hearts, they still dread Loki and his dark powers."

She was trembling like a wind-shaken leaf. I put my arm protectingly around her, and she shivered closer to me in the moonlight. Even the dread that I, too, was feeling could not keep my blood from racing as I looked down at her lovely face. Freya of the White Hands, daughter of the goddess of long ago, Viking maid of the Aesir — I held her in my arms!

I kissed her. As I held her close against my mail coat, the chill wind blew her bright hair across my face.

"Jarl Keith!" she whispered wonderingly.

"Freya," I breathed, "I have never loved any woman before, and I never met you until this day. But now —"

She did not answer me with words. She put her small, strong hands behind my head and drew my lips down again to hers. I felt strangely shaken when I raised my head again. We heard a cough. Frey stood in the pale light near us, regarding us with a half-smile.

"I'll go with my lady Gerda to our castle, kinswoman," he said gently. "No doubt the Jarl Keith would be willing to escort you thither."

When he and Gerda had gone, we followed slowly. My mailed arm was around Freya's slim waist as we walked through the silent, moonlit streets of Asgard. She led me toward the castle on the eastern edge of Asgard. Behind us, Valhalla towered vast and gloomy against the stormy sky. Far to our left gleamed the incredible arch of Bifrost.

"Beloved, I feel armed now against even Loki," whispered Freya happily.

"And I fear only that this is a dream from which I shall awake," I breathed.

We were approaching the dark bulk of the castle that crouched squat and massive on the sheer cliff. A half-dozen blond Aesir warriors were approaching us in the moonlight When they were but a few yards from us, they suddenly drew their swords. Their leader called to them in a fierce undertone.

"That is Freya. She has the key. Seize her, and kill the man!"

CHAPTER VII

Ambush!

THEY SPRANG toward us. Though stupefied by the sudden treachery of Aesir warriors, I retained enough presence of mind to draw my long sword. I pushed Freya aside, struck up a blade that was stabbing at my face. My sword sliced deep into the warrior's neck. His helmet rolled off as he fell, and his yellow hair came off with the helmet!

"These are Jotuns!" I shouted to Freya. "Run and give the alarm!"

I heard her cry pierce the night, but she did not run. A sword-point grazed my shoulder, through my mail. The sting made me yell with rage, and I flung myself at the disguised Jotuns. My whirling blade cut away half the face of one. Another reeled back, clutching an almost severed arm. Then two blades crashed down on my helmet, and I collapsed to the ground.

As I fought to rally my senses, I glimpsed the disguised Jotuns dragging Freya, struggling like a wildcat, toward the cliff. The last thing I remember was trying to rise . . .

The next thing I knew, I was being pulled to my feet. Thor was supporting me, and Frey was examining me with desperate anxiety. Torches flashed as men poured from the nearby castle.

"What happened?" roared the Hammerer. "Where is the lady Freya?"

"Jotuns!" I gasped. "They got into Asgard, disguised as Aesir. They were after the rune key, and must have seen Odin give it to Freya. They seized her and took her that way."

I pointed to the cliffs.

"The stair down to the harbor!" Frey cried. "They must have come in a ship!"

As they rushed forward toward the cliff-edge, I staggered after them. My head still ached from the shock of two swords clashing on my helmet. At the edge of the cliff was the narrow stairway, chiseled down the solid rock of the precipice to the fiord below. Two dead Aesir warriors who lay on the stair showed what had become of the guards. Thor started down the steps, but Frey's heart-stopping shout halted him.

"Look! We are too late!"

Out on the ocean, a ship was forging southward through the raging waves, its sail taut in the screaming winds. It was heading straight along the precipitous coast of Midgard. Swiftly it vanished beyond the cliffs.

"The Jotuns and Freya!" moaned Frey. "They have her and the rune key. Now they can loose dark Loki and bring destruction on Asgard!"

Thor shook his great hammer in terrible rage.

"Loki's work!" he roared savagely. "It was the arch-traitor who put the thought of that cunning ruse into the heads of the Jotuns, by his telepathic tricks."

"Are we just going to stand here?" I cried wildly. "They've got Freya, as well as the rune key."

It was Freya I was thinking of in that moment, rather than the key. Though the key might loose Loki and bring about the final attack on Asgard which the Aesir feared, that possibility was less dire to me than the threat to Freya. To have her snatched from my arms in this very hour when I had won her love! I felt a red fury that made me long to destroy every Jotun in payment for any harm they might do to the Viking maid I loved.

"We can overtake them if we're quick," said Frey. He swung around to the Aesir warriors who had come running from his castle. "Down to the harbor!"

At top speed, we ran down the narrow stairway in the cliff. Thor led, with Frey and me close behind the Hammerer, and a score or more of warriors following. The Moon shone out from behind the flying storm clouds. It lighted our way down the dizzy path that the Aesir had hewn to their harbor. The steps were no more than four feet wide, and there was no protective rail of any kind.

The shouting wind that buffeted us threatened to hurl us off the steps. Below, the black sea thundered, smashing the white foam of bursting waves against the cliffs of Asgard. As we neared the bottom, the steps were so wet with spray that our feet almost slipped from beneath us. Where the stairway ended on the rock ledge that rimmed the harbor, three more Aesir warriors lay dead in their own blood.

"The Jotuns dared do this!" bellowed Thor, his red face dark with rage in the moonlight.

"My own ship!" Frey was shouting above the howling wind to his men. "Cast loose the moorings!"

Dozens of dragon-ships floated in the deep, narrow fiord between the cliffs, moored to iron rings in the ledge. The craft into which Frey leaped was seventy feet long, undecked, and with seats for twenty rowers. Its brazen prow gleamed like a live metal monster. We followed him as the moorings were loosed. The yelling warriors sprang in, taking their accustomed places. Frey grasped the tiller. I stood beside him, while Thor climbed into the bow.

"Push off!" Frey shouted over the roar of breakers. "Up sail!"

Warriors strained their muscles to fend off with long oars. The dragon-ship shot out of the protection of the fiord, into the open sea. Great waves lifted us sickeningly, threatening to hurl us back against the cliffs. But the square, painted sail rose at that moment, as Frey's men frantically pulled the ropes. The wind swung our heavy craft away from the looming cliffs.

The brazen prow buried itself in dark water and came up dripping as vast black waves smashed and lifted us. Cold salt spray dashed our faces. Through the roar and swing of the storm-piled sea, the ship strained southward with increasing speed. The high cliffs of Asgard dropped behind, I glimpsed torches flaring around Valhalla castle as the alarm spread.

We surged past the strait between Asgard Island and the mainland, Midgard. Far overhead, on our left, gleamed the arch of Bifrost Bridge. Then Asgard and Bifrost dropped from sight behind us as our speed quickened. We shot along the mighty cliff coastline of Midgard.

"Can you see them, Thor?" Frey called anxiously to the yellow-headed giant.

His beard glistening with spray as he stood in the plunging and rising bow, Thor was peering ahead.

"Not yet!" the Hammerer roared back against the howling wind.

"What will they do with Freya?" I cried.

Frey shook his head. His handsome face was drawn and desperate beneath his gleaming helmet as he shifted the tiller.

"What will they do to us all, Jarl Keith, if they succeed in using the key to loose Loki? That devil will lead the hosts of the Jotuns in the last terrible attack on Asgard."

"It is all my fault," I said bitterly. "If I had not brought the rune key with me, this never would have happened."

The flying clouds had again obscured the Moon, and black shadow shrouded the stormy sea. Close on our left rose the sinister cliffs of Midgard, soaring sheer from the water. Frey was keeping our ship hazardously near the precipices, to lose no time in the pursuit. So close were we that each mountainous wave threatened to capsize us. The howling winds were bitter cold, freezing the salt spray on our faces. Each time the ship buried its brazen beak in the waves, we shipped water and Frey's warriors were bailing furiously.

A high black promontory jutted from the cliffs ahead, and Frey swung the rudder to carry us outside that rocky point. As the ship heeled around in answer, a smashing mass of icy water almost tore both of us away from the helm. Then we rounded the point, and the Moon broke forth again.

"There they go!" roared Thor's great voice from the bow as the giant Aesir pointed with his hammer.

Far ahead on the wild, moonlit waters, a single ship was flying south along the ominous coast.

"They're heading straight for Jotunheim!" Thor shouted. "We can catch them —"

"Ware ambush!" yelled one of our warriors at that moment.

Simultaneously a shower of arrows rattled down like hail into our craft, instantly killing two of our men. I swung around, appalled. From behind the sharp rock point we had just rounded, a dozen long-ships were darting like ravenous monsters toward us, propelled by bending oars. They were Jotun ships, crowded with huge, black-headed warriors and rowers. Their archers loosed another shower of arrows the instant we discovered them.

"A Jotun ambush!" shouted Frey, swinging the tiller hard. "They knew we'd follow. They waited here for us!"

"Port helm, or they'll grapple us!" bellowed Thor.

It was too late. Next moment, the carved beak of the foremost Jotun ship hit our starboard side with a shock that sent us all staggering. As I scrambled up, I saw steel hooks fly over our gunwale and bite deep into the wood.

"Out swords and cut free!" yelled Frey. I rushed with Frey, stumbling to the side where yelling Jotun warriors were boarding us. We met them at the head of our own men. Swords and axes clashed in front of my eyes. I glimpsed a hairy, brutal face raging toward me behind an upraised ax. Crouching, I thrust hard, felt my sword rip between the lacings of a mail brynja, and bite past into unresisting bone and muscle.

Thor reached our side. Bellowing, he whirled his hammer and crashed it down on Jotun helmets, smashing them and the skulls inside.

Our ship was still being drawn southward by the wind that filled its sail, dragging the Jotun craft that had grappled us. The other Jotun ships were straining oars and sails to grapple with us. The roar of waves under the shuddering ship was drowned by the clash of sword, ax and the terrific clang of Miolnir as the huge hammer crashed down on helmets. Over all rose Thor's terrible battle-cry.

The flat of a Jotun ax struck my shoulder and sent me to my knees. A sword in the hand of a yelling enemy gleamed high above my head. I gaped up, helpless. But Frey stabbed in like a striking serpent. He helped me to my feet as the screaming Jotun toppled overboard.

But a second Jotun craft had maneuvered alongside us. Enemy soldiers were hurling grapples over our port side. Frey sprang to cut them loose, before the hostile reinforcements could board us.

"The Hammerer! Kill the Hammerer!"

Shouting Jotuns leaped upon Thor's towering form like dogs trying to pull down a bear. Miolnir flashed in his hand, almost a thing alive. But two axes crashed on his helmet and he fell, stunned. I was seeking to cut the grapples of our first attacker. My sword slashed the hide ropes. As the Jotun ship was drawn away from us by the waves, I heard a choking cry of despair.

I swung around. Frey had cut the grapples of the other Jotun enemy. But the wild lurch of our ship as it was freed had thrown him into the black waters. He was helplessly sinking, weighted down by his heavy mail coat. Instantly I tore off my own mail coat, flung it away, and dived from the back rail into the sea. The icy shock of waters smashed the breath from my body. As my head broke the surface, I saw the battle that had been carried onward hundreds of yards. The Jotun ships were trying to get their grapples on the Aesir craft again. But the Aesir warriors were dismayed by the stunning of Thor and the loss of Frey. They had swung their ship around and were fleeing back toward Asgard.

I trod water amid the surging waves, looking for Frey. When I glimpsed him going down again, a dozen yards from me, I battled the raving wind and crashing sea until I reached his side. Diving deep, I caught him and pulled him to the surface. It was almost more than I could do to keep him afloat, weighed down as he was by his mail and sword. Now I began to regret taking along my own sword, for it was hampering me. The waves were running mountainously, bearing us in toward the looming cliffs that bulked ominously close.

"Leave me!" Frey choked above the roar of the sea. "Save yourself, Jarl Keith — or we'll both perish."

"Cling to my shoulder — kick hard with your feet," I panted.

His weight threatened to drag me under at any moment. I fought to swim away from the cliffs, but I was like a child in the relentless grip of those great waves.

Then I glimpsed a little beach that indented the cliffs. I recognized it at once. It was the beach where I had landed my plane!

"This way!" I cried to Frey. "We'll be shattered on the cliffs unless we can get to that beach."

The breakers threatened to drag us north of the little sandy indentation. I put my last ounce of strength into swimming obliquely across the thunderous waves. But those boiling breakers carried us resistlessly toward the looming cliff. We were going to be flung against it —

I yelled to Frey and made a convulsive effort. We barely cleared the cliffs, and were washed up to safety on the beach!

CHAPTER VIII

World of Gnomes

FOR SOME minutes we lay on the sand. Though the roaring waves broke over us, neither of us was able to move. Gradually our strength returned, and we dragged ourselves farther up the beach. Frey sat up and panted a question.

"Was Thor slain? I saw him fall as I was hurled into the sea."

"He was only stunned, I think. The men of your ship got it free and fled back toward Asgard."

"I owe you my life, Jarl Keith." Frey's voice throbbed in the darkness. "I was sinking in the waves when you leaped after me. I'll not forget that debt."

I staggered to my feet.

"It's more important that we go after those Jotuns, and rescue Freya and the key."

"By now," muttered the Aesir noble hopelessly, "they must be near Jotunheim. We couldn't overtake them even if we had a ship."

"I can overtake them in a few minutes," I said grimly. "You Aesir may know a lot about atomic fires and subtle forces, but you don't know airplanes. Mine is moored right on this beach."

"Your flying ship?" he gasped. "I had forgotten about it. Is it swift enough to overtake the Jotun ships?"

"Swift enough?" I repeated. "Wait till you get in it. Maybe it'll make you think a little more highly of my science!"

I hastened toward the two great boulders between which I had moored my plane. It was gone! The tracks in the sand showed that it had been dragged down to the water.

"Someone's stolen my ship!" I groaned.

"The Jotuns must have done it. Whoever sent them to kill or capture you, Jarl Keith, sent other warriors later to seize your flying ship."

"They must have dragged it down and pulled it aboard one of their biggest ships," I muttered. "Now we don't have a chance of overtaking Freya's captors before they reach Jotunheim."

"Aye, I fear that all is lost," Frey sighed, "Now that the Jotuns have Freya and the rune key, the Jotun king Utgar will hasten to release Loki from his prison-cave. And once Loki is free and conspiring again with the Jotuns, it will be doom for all Asgard and the Aesir."

My natural inclination was to hasten by the fastest method to Jotunheim, in an attempt to rescue Freya. But I realized that I owed my first duty to the cause of all the Aesir. It was I who had unwittingly brought the rune key that might loose Loki on them.

"Frey, tell me. Where and how far from here is the cave in which Loki is held prisoner?"

"It is miles to the south, deep in the labyrinth of caves that lie under Midgard," he said bewilderedly. "Why do you ask?"

"If you and I hurried to the door of Loki's prison and waited there," I explained eagerly, "we could be there when the Jotun king came to release Loki. We could strike Utgar down and take back the key before he could release that devil. And then, with the key safe, we could find a way to get Freya out of Jotunheim."

Frey was startled by the boldness of my plan.

"It is a daring scheme," he breathed, "and I do not crave to go near Loki. Yet it might succeed. It might prevent his escape."

"How can we get to that prison-cave before the Jotuns get there with the rune key?"

"There's but one quick way — through the tunnels of the Alfings," Frey declared.

"The Alfings? The dwarfs who live in the caves under the mainland?"

"Yes, Jarl Keith, and they like no strangers to come unasked into Alfheim. Yet they are friends of Freya and might let us pass through for her sake. It's dangerous to try, but I am willing."

"Lead on, then," I said. "Find the nearest way into the Alfings' caverns!"

Frey led me to a black opening in the rock wall, the mouth of a pitch-dark passage that ran straight back into the cliff. Its sides showed that it had been excavated by human ingenuity. We entered it.

The tunnel was only five feet high, forcing us to stoop as we proceeded. In a few moments, we were blinded by complete darkness, but we groped on. Then Frey stopped suddenly in the cramped passage. I glimpsed the glimmer of green eyes shining at us from ahead.

"Wild beasts?" I asked, my hand going to the hilt of my sword.

"Alfings," Frey answered tautly. "They can see us even in this darkness. Take your hand from your sword and do not move, lest you die quickly."

I stood unmoving as a statue beside Frey, peering tensely into the darkness ahead, listening to the muffled sound of rapid shuffling. The green eyes shining eerily through the blackness were increased in number. The extreme tension in Frey's figure beside me told me that we were in peril. I remembered what Odin had said of the Alfings. They were an older race than either Jotun or Aesir, and had taken no part in the wars between the two great enemy peoples. "We are friends, Alfings!" Frey called clearly.

From the dark answered a heavy, hoarse, growling voice.

"You come uninvited into Alfheim. The penalty is death, whether you be Jotuns or Aesir."

"We are Aesir," Frey answered quickly, "and we entered your passages only because of dire necessity. I am Frey, kinsman of the lady Freya, whom you know well."

There was a low murmur of deep voices from ahead, as though his statement had caused excitement.

"Freya's name may save us here," he muttered to me. "She has always been a friend of the Alfings, as her mother and mother's mother were before her."

The bass voice answered from the dark.

"The lady Freya is welcome always in Alfheim. But that welcome has not been extended to the other Aesir, as you well know. However, we shall take you to our king Andvar for judgment. Lay down your weapons."

"Drop your sword, Jarl Keith," said Frey.

Our swords fell to the rock floor together. We saw the shining green eyes approach, heard heavy feet thumping all around us and the sudden scratch of flint on steel. A spark leaped. Big resinous torches flamed with ruddy light, illuminating the whole cramped tunnel.

Surrounding us were a dozen Alfings, all armed with short, heavy spears and huge maces of metal. They kept their weapons raised alertly toward us, except the two who held the torches. The tallest was only four-and-a-half feet high. But their bodies were squat and massive beyond belief, with enormously broad, hunched shoulders, arms and legs of tremendous thickness, and big heads with shaggy, dark hair. Their faces were massive and swarthy, their green eyes shining like those of animals. They wore leather tunics and leather sandals soled with iron.

"Andvar will judge you, Aesir," their leader rumbled to us, his green eyes watching us suspiciously. "If you try to escape, you die."

"We have no thought of escape," I assured him. "Lead us to Andvar."

The Alfings shuffled forward with us along the cramped tunnel, one of the torch-bearers keeping ahead and one behind. The others watched us closely, keeping their weapons alertly raised. Presently the tunnel ran into another low passage chiseled from the rock, and then into another.

"Do these people always live underground?" I asked Frey.

"Not all the time, Jarl Keith. They emerge cautiously by day, sometimes. But their dwellings and workshops are in these caves."

"Workshops?" I repeated.

"The Alfings are cunning workers with strange skills," Frey explained. "Not alone are they wonderful forgers of metal. They know how to transmute metals at will, by an alchemy that makes use of radioactive force. Freya has often told me of their weird achievements."

After an Alfing had run ahead to bear tidings of our approach, I heard drums throbbing hollowly through the maze of passages. Ever louder they boomed, like the amplified beating of many hearts. We emerged from the tunnel into a great cavern, one of their smithies. Great forges blazed in it, and clever trip-hammers were beating out white-hot metal.

The quivering glow of the forges paled the torchlight of our guards, and the banging clangor of the brazen hammers was deafening in the echoing cavern. The Alfing smiths looked up from their work to watch with wide, suspicious green eyes. We passed through another resounding cavern of smiths, and entered a chamber that was filled with a glaring white radiance.

"What is that?" I exclaimed, blinking.

"One of the caverns of the alchemists," Frey said. "See, Jarl Keith, how they use strange science to change metals."

A strange science it was, indeed. The primitive science of the dwarfs was accomplishing things beyond the highly advanced science of my modern world. From leaden brackets projecting from the cavern wall were suspended a dozen globes like brilliant, tiny suns, blazing with white radiance. These were bits of extremely active matter procured from far within the Earth by the fearless dwarfs.

Round shields of heavy lead confined the fierce radiation and firmly directed it downward. That intense torrent of force was filtered through varying plates of translucent, quartzlike stone. Thus tempered, the streaming force played upon leaden trays set underneath. On these trays lay iron or copper objects — ornaments, buckles, dagger-sheaths, and the radiation was transforming them into gold!

"These little fellows aren't so primitive," I muttered enviously. "Transmutation of metals by radiation — it's been a laboratory experiment in my own world, but here they actually use it."

"It is quite simple, Jarl Keith," Frey stated. "They get the radio-active matter from the safer fringes of Muspelheim, the fire-world far beneath this land, from which we originally came."

"But what about those plates of quartz they use as filters?"

"They're not really quartz, but a synthetic substance the Alfings can make," he explained. "They can be adjusted to screen out any particular frequency of vibratory force desired. Thus the Alfings are able to apply the isolated radiation which the transmutation needs."

We passed through two more of the alchemic workshops, and then reentered the dark tunnels.

"Frey, will the dwarf king help us?" I asked in a low, anxious voice.

"I don't know," Frey said doubtfully. "He may, if he thinks there's danger of Loki's release. The Alfings fear Loki as greatly as we do."

CHAPTER IX

Loki's Prison

THE DRUMS ahead stopped throbbing. Frey and I were escorted into the greatest cavern, which was bright with the flickering light of many torches. Hundreds of Alfings had hastily gathered here. There were a few of their women, short-statured and hunched as the men, and not many children. Men, women and children all stared at us in heavy silence.

Upon a stone terrace at the end of the cavern stood a massive Alfing who wore a heavy gold collar studded with wonderful jewels. Bright, suspicious and fearful eyes looked at us out of his dark, heavy face. It was Andvar, the Alfing king. He listened to our guards' explanation, then spoke to me in a rumbling bass voice.

"Who are you, stranger? You do not look like any Aesir, yet you claim to be a friend of the lady Freya."

"I'm her betrothed," I declared, "and this is her kinsman Frey."

"The lady Freya alone among Aesir or Jotun is welcome here," Andvar said sullenly. "She alone has always been friendly to us. But you are not welcome. You have trespassed in entering Alfheim."

"Dire necessity forced us to trespass," I said earnestly. "We hurry to reach the deep cavern where Loki lies imprisoned."

My words created a stir of horror among the Alfings.

"Why should you wish to go there?" Andvar demanded. "None of the Aesir has gone to Loki's prison since he was confined there, long centuries ago."

"We must go there," I replied, "because even now the Jotuns will be hurrying by other ways to release Loki. They have abducted the lady Freya, and with her they took the rune key that will unlock the door of Loki's prison."

Cries of fear broke from the throng of Alfings in the torchlit cavern. I saw Andvar's massive face grow pale beneath its swarthy skin.

"They hold the lady Freya and the rune key?" he boomed. "But if they release Loki with the key, it means war again between Jotun and Aesir. This time, Loki might well win the final victory!"

"He might," I agreed quickly. "And if Loki succeeded in conquering the Aesir, he will lead the Jotuns to subdue Alfheim."

The terror upon the faces of the Alfings showed clearly that they had already thought of the possibility.

"There is still time to prevent the freeing of the arch-fiend," I continued. "If we can get to his prison before the Jotuns come there with the key, we can prevent them from setting Loki free. Will you help us?"

Andvar shook his great head troubledly.

"We cannot help you attack the Jotuns. Long ago, we told both Aesir and Jotun that we would have no part in their war, but would live at peace and trade with both of them. We cannot break our promise by raising our weapons against the Jotuns."

"But unless the Jotuns are prevented from freeing Loki, it means war, in which you Alfings may be crushed as between mill-stones! If you strike now to help us, you may save your race. And you will be helping to save Freya, your friend."

Doubt and fear were written on the faces of all the swarthy, stunted Alfings in the torchlight. But as Frey and I waited tensely, Andvar shook his head again.

"We dare not help you. If the Jotuns ever learned that we had raised our weapons against them, then would they seek to destroy us all. They would ruin our gardens and slay our hunters on the surface, and we would not dare emerge any more. Thus would we perish, since we could not live always in darkness."

"It's no use, Jarl Keith," Frey muttered defeatedly. "They're too afraid of the Jotuns to help us in an ambush."

"But they could give us back our swords and lead us by the swiftest way to the door of Loki's prison," I said quickly. "We alone might be able to prevent Loki's release."

Frey nodded eagerly, his eyes burning with sudden impatience to match wits and strength with the enemy.

"Andvar, you can help us without raising your weapons against the Jotuns," I said. "Give us back our swords, and lead us by the shortest route to the door of Loki's prison. We ourselves will undertake to prevent the release of the evil one."

"If the Jotuns learned that we did even that, they would be enraged against us," Andvar mused. "But they cannot learn of it, unless you tell them. Swear that no matter what befalls you, you will not tell of our part in this. Then we will guide you to Loki's cave."

Frey raised his hand. "I swear it by the Norns, the fates who rule all, and by Wyrd, their mother."

Though I repeated the oath, Andvar seemed only partly satisfied.

"It is a great risk we run. But Loki must not again go free to ravage Midgard with war, death and destruction. We will give you back your swords and guide you, Aesir. It rests upon you two alone to prevent the loosing of Loki."

The red torches bobbed as the Alfings turned fearfully to us.

"We are almost to the cavern-prison of Loki," said Andvar. "I fear to go farther."

The Alfing king's massive face was pale, the dread plain in his green eyes. Our three other dwarfed guides were equally terrified.

"You promised to lead us to the door of the prison," I said. "Take us to where we can see it. Then you can return."

Andvar shuddered and hesitantly advanced with his three subjects, though now their steps were slow and reluctant. We were passing through a high, vaulted cavity deep in the rock beneath Midgard. Andvar and the other Alfings had been leading Frey and myself into the maze of natural cavities. Traveling always westward and southward, I judged we were beneath the center of the rocky mainland.

Hours before, we had left the tunnels and work-caverns of Alfheim. These gloomy spaces we now traversed showed no sign of their presence. The stunted men so feared the very name of Loki that they never went near this labyrinth of caves. It was too close to where Loki's body lay in suspended animation.

My brain was feverish with excitement, hope and despair, as Frey and I followed our Alfing guides. I realized miserably that even if we were able to prevent the Jotuns from setting their dread lord free, that would still leave Freya a prisoner in dark and distant Jotunheim. A prisoner — or perhaps a tortured corpse by now . . .

At that thought, I clutched the hilt of my sword with wild passion. The Alfings had given us back our weapons. Upon these two blades we must depend to vanquish the Jotuns who would come with the rune key to release and awaken Loki. It was a desperate course we had charted. But if Frey was right, upon our swords rested the only hope of thwarting the release of the prisoned archdevil.

Andvar led us into a narrow split in the rock. We squeezed through it in single file, bruising our limbs. From this crevice, we emerged into a silent, tomb-like gallery, piled with rocks in fantastic shapes.

"We go no farther!" quavered Andvar. Tremblingly he pointed toward the far end of the great gallery. "There lies the door of Loki's prison!"

I peered between the masses of fallen rock that filled the gallery. Far away, something like a web of shimmering radiance closed a gap in the rock wall.

"Aye, it is the door of the arch-traitor's prison," Frey whispered. "Well do I remember when Odin placed it there, long centuries ago."

"The Jotuns haven't come yet with the key!" I breathed eagerly. "We're in time!"

"Now we leave you, for we will not go nearer Loki," Andvar muttered fearfully. He handed us one of the torches. "If you succeed in preventing Loki's release, you will rescue our friend, the lady Freya?"

The dwarf king's anxiety softened me.

"Be sure we will, Andvar," I promised. "Somehow we'll get her out of Jotunheim."

"She has always been kind to us, as her mother and mother's mother were before her," Andvar declared. "You are lucky to have won her love, stranger."

"I know," I said humbly.

"Hasten, Andvar!" called the other Alfings softly. "The Jotuns may come at any moment."

Andvar heeded their anxious warning, and hurried through the crevice by which we had just come. The thump of their heavy tread died away.

"Can the Jotuns get to Loki's prison without going through Alfheim as we did?" I asked Frey.

"Yes. There are many ways from the surface into these caves, Jarl Keith. The Jotuns will come by one of them."

Holding the torch high, I advanced with Frey through the lofty cavern. A profound silence made the guttering of the torch, even my own breathing, seem loud to my ears.

My heart was pounding as we approached the shimmering door at the end of the cavern. Now I saw that the door was not of matter at all, but of force, that apparently their web of light was probably less vulnerable than any material door could be. It was projected from apertures on either side of the opening. I guessed that hidden inside the rock must be the mechanisms that projected the force. Frey confirmed my guess.

"Odin himself devised the projectors and sunk them in the rock. They are operated by inexhaustible atomic power, and generate an absolute barrier to all three-dimensional matter. They are controlled by the tiny projector in the rune key. That is why, if the key were destroyed, the door would vanish in one terrific flash of force."

With a queer, shrinking dread, I approached the transparent web. I was about to touch it when Frey hastily drew me back.

"Keep a safe distance," he warned. "The extra-dimensional force web would blast your hand."

Shaken, I stood a few feet from the shimmering curtain, peering into the small cave beyond.

"Loki!" I whispered hoarsely.

He lay upon a skin rug, dimly visible in the light of the radiant door. His arms were outspread, his face upturned. Bright gold was Loki's hair and mustache. slender and gracefully formed was his unmoving body. He wore helmet, brynja and sword like those of the Aesir.

Loki's face was — beautiful! Mere handsomeness could never have struck such awe into me. His eyes were closed, the long, golden lashes slumbering on his white cheeks.

"Most beautiful of all the Aesir was Loki outwardly — a fair shell that hid his black, evilly ambitious soul," Frey said fiercely. "See, Jarl Keith. Beside him lie his monstrous pets, prisoned like himself in suspended animation."

I tore my eyes from the angelic face of Loki. When I looked beyond him, I felt the hair of my neck bristle. Upon the rough rock floor of that little cavern crouched a huge gray wolf. Large as a bear, it held its mighty head between its paws, its lips baring the awful fangs in an eternal snarl. In a complete circle around both Loki and the frightful wolf lay the black, motionless coils of an enormous serpent.

"The wolf Fenris and Iormungandr, the Midgard snake!" hissed Frey, his eyes glittering hate. "The pets that Loki cherished, and that were prisoned here with him by Odin's science."

"Whoever heard of a wolf and serpent as big as that?" I gasped.

"Loki made them grow that large, by some scientific means," Frey muttered. "Another of his evil experiments."

"He must have used some form of glandular control," I said thoughtfully. "Loki certainly must have had plenty of scientific knowledge."

For a few moments, we stared at the three fiends in silence.

"Frey, are they really only in suspended animation?" I whispered. "They seem to be dead."

"They are alive," Frey assured me. "Only the functions of Loki's physical body are suspended. His mind is conscious, even at this moment. Just as a man can be paralyzed and still be fully conscious, so it is with Loki."

"But even if he's conscious, how could he have influenced me from afar to keep the rune key? How could he have raised the storm that blew me here, and given orders to the Jotuns to be waiting for me?"

"In his researches, Loki had developed the power to send telepathic messages," Frey explained tautly. "Do your scientists have that power?"

"They're just beginning to find out about it. They call it extrasensory perception."

"Loki had developed that power to great lengths," Frey said. "Though his body is prisoned here, his conscious mind can send forth powerful thought messages. Such commands he sent into your mind, Jarl Keith, from here. And such messages he must have sent to the Jotuns, ordering them to operate his strange mechanisms. They can raise tempests such as blew you here."

"And he's been held here for centuries, with his mind awake and conscious!" I muttered in horror, shuddering. "What is that vapor drifting about the chamber?"

"That contains the secret of suspended animation," Frey told me. "Odin devised the vapor, which freezes and halts the chemical activity of the body's cells, at the same time preserving each cell unharmed. The vapor alone holds Loki and his pets frozen. If the radiant door were opened and the vapor escaped, the arch-traitor and his pets would awake —"

"Listen!" I hissed suddenly, clutching Frey's arm.

I had heard a dim murmur of voices, footsteps approaching from the farther end of the gallery.

"The Jotuns come!" breathed Frey.

"Coming to free Loki!" I said. "We've got to hide, and take them by surprise!"

CHAPTER X

Captive in Jotunheim

I DASHED out the torch and flung it away. We were plunged into darkness that was relieved by only the pearly radiance from the shimmering door of Loki's prison. I pulled Frey behind the shelter of one of the fantastic piles of rocks that littered the cavern. We drew our swords and crouched there, waiting.

The voices and footsteps grew louder. Red torchlight began to gleam vaguely into the dark gallery from the crevice at its far end. Then, as the torch-bearers stepped into the cavern, it blazed with flickering crimson light. There were ten people in the Jotun party. Besides eight big, black-bearded Jotun warriors, three of whom bore torches, there were two leaders.

One was a giant Jotun with a wolf-like, savage face and glittering black eyes. His great helmet and armor were studded with gems, his fierce face blazing with excitement. The other was a dark-haired Jotun woman whose sinuous form was clothed in a long, deep-blue gown. Her dark beauty was striking, but there was something unholy in the avid eagerness of her lustrous black eyes.

"Utgar, the Jotun king," whispered Frey. "And Hel, princess of Jotunheim, past accomplice of Loki in his plots against the Aesir and his pupil in dark scientific knowledge."

"Utgar has the rune key," I muttered, gripping my sword-hilt.

I had seen the little gold cylinder shining in the hand of the Jotun king. From Utgar came a bellow of brute triumph, bestial exultation, as his eyes found the shimmering door at the end of the gallery.

"It is the place!" he shouted. "There's the door of our lord's prison."

Hel, the dark Jotun princess, uttered a low laugh.

"Said I not that I could bring you to the place by ways which would avoid the Alfings?" she asked in a throaty, sinisterly rich voice. "For I myself was guided by the thought message of our lord Loki, who instructed us how to get the key from Asgard —"

Her supple figure stiffened, and her narrowed eyes roved around the torch-lit cavern.

"I hear our lord's mind speaking to me now," she murmured. "He warns that there is danger lurking in this place. Enemies have been here and are still here!"

"Frey, we must strike now," I whispered urgently. "Fell the

torch-bearers, while I strike down Utgar and grab the key. In the darkness, we may be able to escape."

But as we tensed to spring out on the Jotuns, the princess Hel uttered a sharp cry.

"Our enemies are there!" She pointed straight at the rocks behind which we crouched. "Our lord warns —"

Instantly Frey and I leaped out, with our swords flashing in the torchlight. But the split-second warning of Hel had destroyed our advantage of surprise. Just as swiftly, Utgar and his warriors had ripped out their swords. They met us with raised blades as we charged them.

I leaped toward Utgar and my sword slashed desperately. But with a roar of rage, the Jotun king parried my stroke with his own great blade. Numbing shock deadened my arm as my steel clashed against his. Sparks leaped from the blades. Seeking to beat down his guard with terrific strokes and seize the rune key from his hand, I glimpsed Frey in silent action. He was striking down first one of the three Jotun torch-bearers, then another.

The princess Hel had darted out of the path of combat and stood with a tiny dagger in her hand. Her eyes were blazing with excitement. Skilled as Frey was, and regardless of my furious resolve to rescue Freya, we were beset by greater numbers. They began driving us back.

"It is Frey and the outlander!" Utgar bellowed as he fought off my attack. "Separate them and cut them down!"

"Kill them!" Hel commanded throatily. "They seek to prevent the freeing of our lord!"

With a strength that was born of desperation, I beat down Utgar's sword. My blade whirled up and I yelled hoarsely as I set myself to cleave the neck of the Jotun king.

"Jarl Keith, look out behind!" shouted Frey, though he was hard-pressed by three antagonists.

I heard a sword swish down behind me. I started to spin around, but the blade descended on my helmet with stunning force. My brain rocked, and bursting light blinded me.

I felt myself falling, my sword dropping from my nerveless hand, my vision beginning to darken. I glimpsed two Jotuns leaping upon Frey's back as he fought. Striking him with daggers, they dragged him down at last, covered with blood.

"Now give me the rune key, Utgar!" I heard Hel cry. "I'll release our lord before other Aesir come to stop us."

"Aye, set Loki free at once!" Utgar bellowed, his brutal, dark face triumphant as he handed her the golden cylinder.

Dimly, while I fought to retain consciousness, I saw Hel glide forward to the shimmering door of Loki's prison, the rune key in her hand. I saw her point the golden cylinder toward the shimmering web. When she pressed the graven runes upon it in a complex combination, the door began to fade!

"Our lord's mind instructed me well how to operate this key that Odin's science devised!" gloated Hel.

The web of force was gone. The projectors which had maintained it had now been turned off by the operation of the rune key. Out of the cave within rushed a cloud of pale-green vapor. Hel recoiled from it. Utgar, too, staggered back, choking and dazed. My consciousness was passing.

Darkly I perceived the prostrate body of Loki stirring. I saw him stumble to his feet. The huge wolf Fenris was rising, opening blazing, feral eyes, snarling a savage roar that reverberated thunderously. And the coils of the giant serpent were sliding slowly in reawakened life.

Loki stepped out of the chamber in which he and his monstrous companions had been imprisoned so long in suspended animation. As he stood, his tall, slender, graceful form seemed to expand. His beautiful white face and gold hair shone in the torchlight.

Blazing like those of Lucifer newly risen from the pit, those dazzling eyes swept over the awed, trembling Jotuns, the prone forms of Frey and myself, the stupefied and dread-shadowed face of Utgar, the unholy eagerness of Hel's dark, beautiful face. Tangible light and force seemed to flame from Loki's blue eyes.

Beside Loki, the wolf Fenris was snarling horribly at us. Its terrible white fangs were bared, its huge head thrust forward with ears flattened. And on the arch-traitor's other side reared up the great spade-shaped head of the Midgard snake. Cold reptilian eyes glittering, the forked red tongue flickered in and out between its scaly jaws.

Darkness was claiming my mind. As though from dim, enormous distances, I heard the jubilant, golden voice of Loki.

"Free at last! Now comes the hour of my vengeance upon the Aesir!"

That voice was the last thing I heard. Even as its accents of superhuman triumph struck my ears, complete unconsciousness claimed me.

A throbbing, blinding pain in my head was my first sensation of returning consciousness. Then I became aware that I lay upon a hard bed of some kind, and that the air was cold and damp. I tried to open my eyes and could not. Summoning strength by a great mental effort, I raised my hand weakly to my head. Instantly I heard a joyful, sweet voice.

"He awakens, Frey!"

That voice, vibrating through the fibers of memory in my dazed brain, compelled me to open my eyes. Freya was bending over me. Her pale, beautiful face was framed by her unbound yellow hair, and it was eager with gladness. Her warm, blue eyes looked fondly down into mine.

She still wore the white linen gown that she had worn at the feast in Valhalla, before her abduction. And I saw, too, that Frey, pale, and bandaged around his neck and shoulder, had stumbled over to look down at me.

"Freya!" My voice was only a weak whisper.

Tears were in her lovely eyes as she put her face against mine, her cool cheek against my lips.

"Jarl Keith!" she whispered. "I feared you were dying. It has been hours that you have slept like the dead."

Weakly I put my arms around her slim shoulders and held her close to me. The bright gold of her hair on my face seemed at that moment to hold all of the sweetness in the world.

Then I looked beyond her: Frey's pale, haunted face and terrible remembrance rushed through my stunned mind. Loki and Fenris wolf and the great serpent emerging from their prison!

"Loki!" I gasped. "I saw him come forth —"

"Yes, Jarl Keith," said Frey. "That which we Aesir have feared for centuries has happened. the arch-devil has been released."

The blood seemed to leave my head as realization crashed home. The ancient rhyme on the rune key seemed to echo mockingly in my ears.

> *Bring me not home,*
> *Lest Ragnarok come.*

It had happened. I had brought the fateful rune key home. And now Loki and his monsters were free to lead the Jotun hosts in the last and most terrible attack against Asgard. I groaned at the thought of my own guilt, for it was all my responsibility. It was I, inspired by what spells of Loki I could not imagine, who had caused the rune key to be found. I had brought it into this hidden land to loose an incredibly evil menace that had lain dormant for centuries — yet conscious to add new torments and more vicious horrors to the old ones.

Freya had raised her face. She was looking at me with blue eyes that were bright with dread, her red lips quivering.

"But where are we?" I cried, trying to sit up. "How is it you're with us, Freya?"

"We are in Jotunheim, Jarl Keith," she whispered. "I have been held here since the Jotun raiders brought me here and took the rune key away. And you and Frey were brought here and prisoned with me but a few hours ago. You were unconscious — dying, I feared."

Her slim arm supported me as I sat up. Dazedly I stared around. We occupied a small stone cell, with walls that were of massive, damp blocks. The heavy wooden door was solidly closed. One tiny, barred window admitted pale daylight and barely enough air. Frey and Freya helped me as I rose to my feet from the rude hide couch where I had lain. I stumbled with their support to the window, and looked out at ancient Jotunheim.

Jotunheim crouched like a great, slumbering reptile on a low plateau above steaming marshes. A sluggish, black river wound from the rugged hills behind the city. Down past the stone walls, it oozed through the dank, brooding marshes to the distant sea.

It was a city of squat, massive castles and forts, built with antediluvian rudeness. The giant stone blocks were overgrown with green, hideous moss. Our cell was in the basement level of the most enormous of the castles, a high, oblong structure.

Even in daylight, the city was filled by chill, foggy mists from the streaming morasses below. From our window I could see scores of longships moored in the river which wound past Jotunheim's northern wall. Hosts of Jotuns were busy on ships and shore. Warriors and thralls were carrying stacks of weapons, fitting new oars and masts, all in a bustle of hurried activity. Through the ancient, somber city trotted squads of hastening warriors, hurrying men and women. Everyone was feverishly engaged in mysterious preparations.

"Captives in Jotunheim," I moaned. "And Loki —"

"He is here, too," Frey said unhappily. "In this palace, which belongs to Utgar, he directs the preparations you see. Those are the preparations for the last great attack on Asgard."

Freya, holding my arm, looked up at me with blue eyes that were almost black with dread.

"The Jotuns went mad when Loki arrived with Utgar, Hel, you and Frey," she said. "They cry that now at last shall they wipe the Aesir from existence."

"Ragnarok, the final struggle, draws near," Frey declared solemnly. "Aye, this is the struggle that we Aesir knew must come if ever Loki were freed."

"But Odin and the Acsir will not yield!" I cried. "They will throw back Loki and the Jotuns!"

"I pray the fates that it be so," Frey said. "But the Jotuns out-number us how more greatly than before. With Loki and his evil science, Fenris and Iormungandr fighting on their side, we have reason to fear for Asgard. But if perish we must, the Jotuns and Loki shall perish with us. That I know."

"Can't we sneak out of here and get back to Asgard?" I asked urgently.

His haggard face twisted into a hopeless smile.

"How could we even escape this cell? And if we did, the whole city is swarming with armed warriors making ready. Never could we win past all the soldiers of Jotunheim to freedom."

"What will they do with us?" I pressed. "Why do they hold us instead of killing us?"

"I don't know," he muttered. "Be sure that Loki has some evil scheme in mind that will make use of us."

He staggered, and I hastened to help him to the hide couch, where he sat down weakly.

Frey's wounds in that battle in the cave had been serious ones. He had lost most of his unaging strength.

My own strength was rapidly returning. I had paced back and forth from door to window of the cell, racking my brain for some means of escape. There was none. Finally I gave it up and sat dully down beside Freya.

Hours must have passed as we sat in a heavy, hopeless silence. The Sun was setting through the slowly thickening mists of Jotun-heim, casting a pale beam onto the stone floor. There was a rattle at the lock of our door. It opened, and a big, fierce-eyed Jotun captain stood glaring at us. Behind him were a dozen guards.

"You, outlander," said the captain to me. "Come with us. Our lord Loki would speak to you."

'What does Loki want with me?" I demanded, rising painfully to my feet.

"Is it for me or for you, outland dog, to question the reasons of our lord?" roared the captain. "Come, or be dragged!"

I pressed Freya's hand and went with the guards. In a gloomy, stone corridor, they bared their swords to cut me down if I at-tempted escape or resistance. The door of the cell was barred again, and two of the Jotuns took their places outside it. The others marched me away.

The dank chill of the passage struck me to the marrow. But I felt a greater chill of dread at this summons from Loki. I was going to face the arch-traitor who had waked for his final most vicious revenge . . .

CHAPTER XI

The Arch-fiend

WE PASSED through gloomy corridors and chambers of age-old stone, crusted with evil-looking white fungi and lichens, dripping with condensed vapor. Rats squeaked across our path unheeded. Up broad stairs of troglodytic hugeness, we climbed into the upper levels of the massive palace. Everywhere we met soldiers and thralls hurrying to and fro, carrying piles of spears and arrows, stacks of shields, and other war supplies.

Tense preparations for the attack on Asgard were unceasingly going on through the whole palace and city. The Jotun captain led us through another corridor, to the edge of a large, poorly lit hall.

"Wait," he barked, stopping. "Our lord is not finished with Princess Hel."

"What are they doing?" I asked, awed. "What kind of machinery is that?"

"Silence, outlander!" snapped the captain.

I stood among my guards, staring at the amazing scene that was taking place. The hall into which I looked was of great dimensions, its roof supported by a forest of massive stone pillars. The only illumination came from pale shafts of daylight that trembled down from small, high, slit-windows, as though afraid to enter this dark place. White wisps of fog still swirled amid the pillars, like homeless ghosts idly drifting.

On a raised stone platform at one end of the hall, in a massive throne carved of black rock, sat Loki. His bright golden hair glittering in the gloom, and the flashing mail he wore made him seem a figure of living light. Beside his throne, mighty head between its paws, lay the monster wolf Fenris. The Midgard snake I did not see.

Loki's beautiful face was intent, his graceful form leaning forward. Beside his throne stood the big, black-haired Jotun king Utgar, and the darkly beautiful Hel, princess of Jotunheim. They were staring into an unfamiliar-looking mechanism whose complexities of glowing wires and glass rods were partly hidden by a metal cover. On the cover, though, was a square quartz screen that reproduced a living scene.

"See, lord Loki, the picture clears!" cried Hel.

"I see, too," Utgar roared. "It is Asgard!"

"Aye, it is Asgard," said Loki in his wonderfully sweet voice, his eyes brooding as he peered into the screen. "Behold, the nobles of the Aesir are gathered in Valhalla for council. We shall hear them."

Loki touched another control. From the great hall's edge, I could barely detect a low buzz of speech from the mechanism.

"I cannot hear clearly," Utgar complained. "What are they saying?"

"The king Odin is speaking," said Hel, with a contemptuous smile on her beautiful face. "He tells the Aesir nobles that he fears Loki is loosed, with Fenris and Iormungandr, and that Frey and Freya and the outland Jarl are captives in Jotunheim. The Aesir look wildly at one another, at that news. There is a shout from Thor."

"That stupid, brainless bear!" said Loki scornfully. "A lout who knows nothing but wrestling, eating and cracking skulls."

"What says the Hammerer?" Utgard asked.

Hel laughed. "The lord Thor is angry. His head is bound from a wound, as you can see. He roars that the Aesir vanquished Loki and the Jotuns once before, and that they will do so again. And this time, he says, they will slay Loki instead of prisoning him."

Loki leaped to his feet. A flash of rage as blinding and terrible as lightning twisted his face.

"Slay me?" he hissed. "Sons of the Aesir, my ancient people, you will rue that thought when Asgard goes down in flame and death."

"The king Odin is speaking again," Hel told Utgar. "He says they must prepare for the coming struggle. They must devise, if possible, some way to rescue Frey and Freya and the Jarl Keith from Jotunheim. And Odin says he fears Loki may be using his scientific powers to spy on them. He will make sure, he says —"

Hastily Loki reached out and touched a screw on that strange mechanism. The picture in its quartz screen and the buzz of voices ceased. I knew it must be some super-development of television, able to operate without a transmitter.

"We have seen and heard enough," Loki said moodily. "The Aesir know we will attack them, but they'll have small time to prepare. Two days hence, we march on Asgard to crush them."

"Aye, but be careful, lord," warned Utgar anxiously. "Odin, too, has great powers of ancient science. Once before, he snatched victory from us because of your too great confidence."

"Croak not your warnings to me!" Loki stormed. "I have had centuries in which to think. Nothing can save the Aesir this time. Get you both gone now, till I call you."

At the tone of his master's voice, Fenris raised his enormous head and snarled horribly. Utgar hastily retreated from Loki's blazing wrath, backing toward a door. Less urgently the princess Hel followed him. Without looking in the direction where I stood with my guards, watching this scene in fascinated horror, Loki spoke.

"Bring the outlander before me."

As the Jotuns marched me forward I saw that they were all trembling. They halted me in front of the black throne. I looked up defiantly into the brooding blue eyes of Loki. He spoke finally to the captain of the Jotun guards.

"Take your men and wait outside the hall."

"But, lord, we can't leave you here alone with this outland dog!" protested the captain.

Loki turned a withering glance on him.

"Think you I need such as you to protect me?" he asked bitingly. "Get you gone!"

The captain and his men almost tumbled over themselves in their haste to leave the hall. I stood there alone, facing Loki, the wolf, the snake that had slid to the throne, in that vast and gloomy hall of drifting fog and chill. Uncontrollably my heart pounded in sudden excitement and hope.

For my eyes had fastened on the sword that hung at Loki's side. If I could end the arch-traitor's life with that thirsty blade, I would die gladly, knowing that I had atoned for bringing the rune key into peaceful Asgard.

I sprang forward with wild determination. But instantly, like a thunderbolt of hurtling flesh, the huge wolf Fenris leaped upon me. The monster's weight knocked me to the floor. His huge, hairy body crushing me, his hot breath scorching me and terrible fangs gleaming, I saw Fenris' mighty jaws yawning above my face.

The glaring, feral green eyes of the gigantic wolf blazed down into mine with almost human hatred. Those jaws gaped to crush my skull like an eggshell.

"Fenris, loose him!" snapped Loki's voice, coming as though from a great distance.

Fenris turned his massive head a little, and a protesting, savage snarl rumbled from him. He was resisting his master's order. He wished to kill me.

"Do you grow disobedient?" flared Loki's voice.

I heard his quick step coming from the throne toward me. Still pinned down by Fenris' huge weight, I saw Loki reach down and smack the wolf stingingly on its great muzzle.

Fenris whimpered apologetically to his master. The wolf backed off hastily. As Loki went back and seated himself again on the black throne, the huge animal again crouched down beside it. But his feral, blazing eyes never left my face. Shaking, I stumbled to my feet. I saw amusement in the brilliant blue eyes and angelic face of Loki as he sat regarding me.

"Do you still wish to kill me, outlander?" he asked with a shockingly sweet laugh. "I might not be able to hold Fenris from your throat, next time."

Hearing his name, the monstrous wolf growled deep in his throat, snarling and baring his great fangs as he watched me. Hot resentment at the mocking devil who was regarding me with such amusement made me stiffen and clench my fists.

"If you are going to have me killed, why not get it over with?" I demanded.

"I am not sure that I shall take your life, outlander," said Loki, searching my face. "After all, I owe you much. It was you who brought back into this land the rune key that finally gave me and my pets our freedom."

"I wish I had died before your hideous mental commands seduced my brain!"

"Now why should you wish that?" Loki asked with deep interest. "Why should you hate me so?"

"Because I know that you are evil and that your plans are vicious," I said harshly. "For twenty centuries in the outside world, the name of Loki has been synonymous with treachery, even though no one in that outer world dreams that a real Loki ever existed."

Loki nodded his golden head thoughtfully.

"That is true. Yet what evil have I done to you, Jarl Keith? Have I not brought you into a land that no other of your race has ever seen? Have I not given you new and undreamed-of adventure? What more could I do for you? You see, I know that in your soul you are an adventurer, a seeker of the new and the strange."

"It's what you plan to do to the Aesir that makes me hate you," I retorted. "I admire them — and you plot to use the Jotuns to destroy them."

Loki's beautiful face darkened, like the Sun when a storm cloud veils it. His wondrous eyes throbbed with an age-old hate.

"I loved the Aesir, too, Jarl Keith," he said broodingly. "Yes, long ago when we dwelt in deep Muspelheim and I was second to Odin himself, I did much for my race. I delved into scientific secrets that had been hidden from them, and I found new truths. I would have done much more for them, had they made me their ruler in Odin's place. For I was never satisfied, as Odin was, with a static, stagnant well being.

"I burned with the desire to acquire all knowledge that man could acquire, to know the reason for every phenomenon in the world and in the sky. I longed to acquire every power that man ever could acquire, so that we should be unchallenged masters of all nature. It was I who freed the Aesir from sickness and age. I made them almost immortal, by kindling the atomic fires whose radiation prevents disease and age. Was that not a great gift I made to my people?"

As a scientist, I could not help feeling a certain sympathy with Loki. Yet I realized that he was presenting merely his own side of the case.

"Yes," I admitted. "But in making the Aesir that gift of near-immortality, you almost destroyed them. You brought catastrophe on the subterranean world of Muspelheim, and forced them to flee up here. No wonder Odin forbade you to carry on such dangerous researches!"

Loki shrugged. "There can be no great victory without great danger, outlander. I had a vision of leading the Aesir to undreamed-of heights of power and wisdom, though by a road beset with vast perils. I was willing to risk those perils, to be great or to die. But dull Odin blocked my path. He said: 'It is not good to endanger all the world to gain power and learning for ourselves.'

"The Aesir agreed with him, and turned from me and my vaulting dreams. I would have made them like eagles soaring into the sky. But they preferred to follow Odin and live out their lives in dull, accustomed routine."

Loki's eyes blazed, and his graceful form stiffened on the black throne as he spoke. And I could not help feeling sympathy with him. No real scientist could willingly submit to suppression of his desire to know, his yearning to master the laws of nature. Loki's blue eyes fastened on me, and he smiled thoughtfully, his passion fading.

"I read your mind, Jarl Keith," he said quickly, "and I see that you think the same as I."

"Not your lust for power," I snapped.

"Do not deny it," he said. "You are of my own breed, Jarl Keith. We are more alike than any others in this land. For just as I risked my own fate and that of my people to win new knowledge and power, so you, who are also a scientist and searcher after truth, came northward into danger and hardship to search for new, strange truth. Yes, we two are of the same minds."

Though his voice rang with sincerity, I fought mentally against his seductive thoughts.

"It is because we are so much alike," he continued, "that I was able to fling the web of my suggestion into your brain. Though you were far away on your ship beyond the ice, yet I could direct you to recover the sunken rune key."

"How could you do that, Loki?" I asked with intense interest. "How could your will range far when your body was held in suspended animation in that prison-cave?"

"You outlanders have concentrated more on mechanical devices than on the subtler forces of science. Otherwise, you would understand better the nature of the mind. The brain is really an electro-chemical generator, and thought is the electric current it generates. A brain which has developed the power can fling its web of electric thought-impulses abroad and into another brain. It can see with the senses of that other brain and even somewhat direct its physical body.

"Thus, during the centuries that I lay prisoned and helpless, I sent the web of my thoughts far afield, seeking a means of escape. At long last, I located the rune key where the Aesir had thrown it in the outer ocean. I could not send any of the Jotuns to secure it, for they could not cross the vast ice without perishing. But at last your ship came north and was near the sunken rune key.

"I seized the opportunity to influence you to have the rune key dredged up. And once you had it, and were in the air in your flying ship, I sent a mental message to the princess Hel, my pupil, I commanded her to operate the storm-cones in my laboratory, which would cause a tempest to blow you hither."

"Storm-cones?" I repeated. "What device could be used to cause such a tempest?"

Loki smiled and rose to his feet.

"Come, Jarl Keith, I'll show you. I think you, a scientist like myself, will be interested in my laboratory."

CHAPTER XII

The Laboratory

HE LED the way across the vast, many-pillared hall. The giant wolf, Fenris, rose and followed us on padding feet, its feral green eyes never leaving me. Loki brought me into a smaller stone chamber. It was indeed a laboratory — the strangest I had ever seen.

Two small, blazing suns of radioactive matter, suspended in lead bowls, illuminated the dusky room. The intense white radiance glittered off an array of unfamiliar mechanisms and instruments.

I saw another of the complex instruments of remote vision, with a square quartz view-screen, such as Loki, Utgar and Hel had been using in the great hall. And I noticed devices which appeared to be similar to the transmutation apparatus used by the Alfings. But these were greatly refined in design. Using concentrated beams of radioactive energy shot from leaden funnels, they could effect even more rapid transmutation of small metal objects.

Loki led the way to the most striking feature of this array of alien scientific instruments. Proudly he gestured at a row of big objects which looked like heavy nozzles of fused quartz mounted on swivels above square, copper-shielded mechanisms. The interior complexities I could not see. Loki laid his hand on one of the nozzles of quartz.

"These are the storm-cones I long ago devised, Jarl Keith. They can cause the most terrific tempest at a distance of hundreds of miles."

"How can they do that?" I asked incredulously.

"It is quite simple." He smiled. "A lightning storm is caused by a sudden sharp difference in electric potential between cloud and Earth, or cloud and cloud. These storm-cones spray a carefully aimed and canalized electric field that causes such an abnormal difference of potential in any desired location. When I lead the Jotun horde to attack Asgard, I'll first bring destructive lightning down upon the Aesir forces. Then they'll fall easy prey to my savage warriors."

I was too appalled by that threat to comment. Loki led me toward a door on the opposite side of the laboratory.

"Now perhaps you can instruct me a little, Jarl Keith," he said. "Come with me."

The door opened into a big, stone-paved court outside the ancient citadel. It was walled, but a great gate in one wall was open, leading out onto the slope that ran steeply toward the river. Dusk had fallen, and the white mists that shrouded Jotunheim were thicker.

My eyes flew to a familiar object in this court. It was my rocket ship. It had not been destroyed, after all.

"Yes, it is your flying ship," Loki said. "After you landed in Midgard, I knew it was only a matter of days until I was released. I sent a thought order to the princess Hel to have Jotun ships brings the craft here, for I wish much to examine this product of the outland world's science. But don't cherish any hopes of making a sudden escape in it, Jarl Keith. I've only to say a word to send Fenris ravening at your throat."

The monster wolf behind us snarled again, as he heard his name. I shrugged.

"I wouldn't leave without Freya and Frey, anyway."

Loki inspected the whole interior of the plane, asking me quick, intelligent questions about every feature of it. He seemed to grasp the design of the ship and its highly improved rocket motor almost instantly.

"You are clever, you outlanders, to devise such things," he said with sincere respect.

"Don't you want to look at the controls?" I asked.

My heart was thudding, for I had seen a wild, insane opportunity. Loki entered the cabin, and I explained the controls. Then I opened the sack of white chemicals which we always carried on these Arctic flights. I took out a handful and showed them to him.

"These are chemicals that generate heat. We use them to free the plane's wheels if they become frozen into the ice."

"That, too, is clever," he mused as he emerged from the plane. "You outlanders are indeed mechanically ingenious, though you have not probed the ancient science of the deepest forces of nature as we Aesir did."

He said nothing more as he brought me back through the laboratory to the dusky great hall. Fenris stalked at our heels. Then Loki turned.

"I could teach you our ancient science, Jarl Keith," he said, to my surprise. "You could learn much that your science puzzles over. And you would be second only to me, once the Aesir are conquered."

I began to understand what he was suggesting.

"You want me to turn against the Aesir — against my friends?"

"That woman Freya — and even Frey, if you wish — can be spared."

"Why do you wish me to become your follower?" I asked suspiciously.

Loki's beautiful face was undeniably sincere as he answered me.

"Because it is as I said. We two are more akin than any others in this land. We seek scientific truth and love the new and strange. Besides, I have no human friend, for Utgar is but a brute-brained tool, and Hel is but a wicked wildcat who never can learn my science. It is true that I have Fenris and Iormungandr. My wolf and serpent have wisdom and cunning which are almost human, but they are not human friends. Speak, Jarl Keith. Will you join me as friend and follower?"

Stunned by the offer, I tried desperately to think. If I could make Loki believe I was willing to join him, and then work against him —

"Your words are convincing," I answered as though deeply thoughtful. "We are alike. I think that I shall join you, Loki. Loki smiled at me; a weary, half-scornful, half-amused smile.

"Jarl Keith, I thought better of you than to expect you to try such transparent stratagems as this upon me," he said. "Can you not understand that in experience you are to me but as a small child? Can you hope to dupe me when I can read your mind?"

I looked up at him defiantly.

"I would fight the devil with fire. You know the truth now, Loki. I have only hate for you, as for all traitors. You prepare to lead these savage Jotuns against your own people, because your own kind has cast you out."

I know that got under his skin, for his eyes narrowed. His mouth tightened, and for a split-second I glimpsed that angelically beautiful face warp into a hell mask of white fury. It was as though the raging evil inside him looked forth naked and unhidden. The wolf Fenris, as though understanding his master's mood, sprang to his feet and snarled viciously at me. Then Loki's face cleared, and he laughed at me without a trace of ill-feeling.

"You have courage, Jarl Keith, proving even more that you are like myself. Yes, you are afraid to admit to yourself how much we two are alike, and how much you like me."

That shot got home to me, for I sensed that it was the truth. I did feel a sympathy for this fallen Lucifer that was hard for me to thrust down.

"You shall stay prisoned here in Jotunheim until after our forces have conquered Asgard," Loki decided. "Once the Aesir are destroyed and the past cannot be recalled, I think you will be wise enough to join me as friend and follower." He raised his voice in a peremptory order. "Guards, return this prisoner to his cell!"

The Jotun captain and his men came running from outside. Not daring even to look up at their overlord, they hustled me out of the hall.

As I went with them, I looked back. Loki seemed already to have forgotten me. He sat in that dismal, mist-filled hall, brooding with chin in hand, his bright-gold head bent. The wolf Fenris looked up at him with faithful, brilliant green eyes.

I was conducted back through the same dank corridors and passages to the subterranean level of the palace. The tall guards clanked toward the door of our cell and opened it. Without ceremony, I was thrust in. When the door was locked after me, the guards marched away.

Freya came anxiously across the dark little cell and found her way into my arms.

"I feared that you would not return, Jarl Keith," she moaned softly.

"What did Loki want with you?" Frey asked, his pale face intent.

I told them most of what had taken place. Freya listened with horror-widened eyes, her kinsman in thoughtful silence.

"So Loki wishes you to join him," he muttered, when I had finished. "That is strange."

"I think it's only because he's lonely," I said. "He has nothing but contempt for these Jotuns, whom he means to use merely to crush the Aesir. I felt a little sorry for him."

Freya stared at me surprisedly. Frey's pale, handsome face tightened as he warned me.

"Heed not the arch-traitor's subtle persuasions, Jarl Keith! Never lived anyone who could harm man or beast by his silver tongue and handsome face as can Loki."

"Never fear," I reassured him. "My loyalty is with the Aesir. No tempting could ever change that."

I went on to tell them of what Loki had told me in his laboratory, explaining his intention to use his storm-cones against the Aesir.

"We must get back to Asgard and warn Odin, so he can prepare a defense," I concluded. "My flying ship is in the court on the citadel's riverside —"

"How can we reach your craft when we can't even get out of this locked cell?" Frey replied hopelessly.

"I think we can escape this cell, at least," I said. I drew from my pocket a handful of white chemical powder and showed it to them. "It's the chemical I always carried in my plane to melt ice from the wheels when necessary. I showed Loki this handful and then put it in my pocket."

"What good will that do, Jarl Keith?" Freya asked, puzzled.

"The lock on the door of this cell is a crude one, made of soft copper," I answered. "I believe this substance can burn away enough of the lock to free us. I'm going to try it anyhow."

I stuffed the chemical powder into the large crevices of the clumsy lock. Then I took our jar of water and poured a little over the powder. The hissing and sizzling of the chemical reaction continued for several minutes. When it ceased, I gently tugged at the lock. It still held. I pulled harder, and with a rasp, it gave way.

"Follow me," I whispered tensely. "I think I know the direction to the court where the plane is. If we only can get through the corridors without meeting anyone!"

We emerged into the dusty stone passage. I led the way toward the right, taking the first cross-corridor that led northward. The cold chill of the night fog penetrated the marrow of our bones, and our nerves were harp-string taut as we pressed on through the dark corridors.

Suddenly I shrank back into the shadows. I had seen two Jotun warriors approaching from a cross-corridor ahead.

"Hurry!" one was urging the other fearfully. "Do you wish to meet the hideous one that now lurks in these passages?"

"Frey, we'll have to jump them," I whispered. "Be ready."

The two Jotuns came around the corner into our dusky corridor. Frey and I leaped on them, taking them utterly by surprise. What followed was not pretty. We had grabbed their throats, for it was essential that they should not give an alarm. There was a fierce, deadly scuffle in the misty, dark tunnel, until we throttled them.

The Jotuns lay limp when Frey and I straightened, panting. We took the swords the two warriors had not had a chance to draw.

"Come on," I panted. "This way. Those warriors must have entered from one of the outside courts."

We hurried down the shadowy passage from which the Jotuns had come. Then Freya suddenly stopped, pulling me to a halt.

"Listen, Jarl Keith," she urged in a hushed voice. "Something sinister is coming."

In the silence, I heard a strange, silky, rustling sound in the dark and misty passage ahead. It was growing nearer, louder —

A giant, spade-shaped head reared out of the curling mists ahead of us! Two opaline, unwinking eyes that held the dull glitter of an alien intelligence contemplated us from above a gaping mouth in which a forked red tongue flickered.

"This is what the Jotuns feared!" Frey cried wildly.

"The fates save us!" Freya prayed. "It is Iormungandr."

I also recognized that giant, scaly body of long, rippling blackness, that huge head and those alien, glittering eyes. It was Iormungandr who towered before us in the misty dusk of the chill tunnel. The ageless and undying, the great Midgard serpent itself, was glaring down with blood-lusting eyes!

CHAPTER XIII

Flight and Death

WE STOOD petrified by horror in that foggy, stone-walled corridor, gazing cataleptically at the hideous creature whose reptilian head was rearing up from the curling white mists. Freya's slim figure had shrunk against me with a choking cry. Frey stood in front of us, his sword raised, his face wild as he looked up at the looming head.

The hideous, abnormally huge coils could only be glimpsed in the mists beyond. But the giant spade-shaped head that hung above us was clear to our appalled vision. The enormous, opaline eyes were coldly brilliant as they stared down at us.

In that moment of stupefying horror, I recognized the intelligence in those unwinking reptilian eyes. This ser- pent of a bygone age had lived on for centuries in this land of eternal youth, with its master Loki and wolf Fenris. It had acquired an intelligence comparable with the human. A strange mind shone from those coldly malignant eyes.

"The Midgard snake!" Frey whispered.

"Jarl Keith!" Freya screamed to me.

The great head of the snake Iormungandr abruptly darted toward us. Frey struck out madly with his sword. I saw the blade slash into the scaly neck. But it caused only a shallow wound from which merely a little black blood oozed.

The Midgard serpent recoiled, however. Its opaline eyes flamed with rage. From the jaws of the monster, with a terrific hiss, came a cloud of fine green spray that flew toward Frey. He reeled back, covered by that weird vapor. But I leaped forward, dragging him and Freya ahead. I saw our single chance. The momentary recoil of the serpent had left open the mouth of a corridor on the right!

"Quick!" I cried, pulling them toward the black passage.

Frey seemed blinded by the green spray of the serpent. The monster's vast coils were twitching with rage, its head swaying angrily forward again. But we plunged safely into that branching corridor. It was utterly dark. As we stumbled forward in it, I heard a distant babble of alarm from the upper levels of the Jotun palace.

"The Jotuns will be after us," I cautioned. "Loki will be warned of our escape."

"Jarl Keith, Iormungandr follows us!" Freya cried wildly.

The angry hiss of the giant serpent was echoing from the stone walls. And I could hear the loud rustle and scrape of its scaled body as it glided into the dark passage after us.

No more than a few moments could have passed before we reached the end of the passage. But it seemed ages that we ran in blind, unreasoning terror. Slipping on the mossy, wet stone floor, we could hear the clamor of the far-off alarm grow louder and the hissing rustle of the Midgard snake overtaking us.

Then I collided with a metal door that closed the end of the passage. My heart throbbed as if it would burst as I clawed frantically for the knob. If it were locked, if we were trapped here by the serpent —

My hand found the catch, and I tore the door open. Outside was the open air. We stared at the night that was filled with curling white fog-mists through which shone the ghostly Moon. I pulled Freya and the stunned Frey through and slammed the door shut behind us. The catch fell. Next moment, there was a loud thump against the other side of the door as the Midgard snake's huge head struck it.

We had emerged into one of the courtyards of the great palace. In the vague mists, the squat, brutal bulbs of Jotunheim's structures rose darkly all around us. But now torchlight was flashing from the upper windows of the palace as the alarm spread.

"Which way?" Frey mumbled thickly, gaping about in the shrouding mists, his sword in his unnerved hand.

"This way," I said decisively, leading them toward the left. "It's the next court."

Then I heard the stamp of restless horses on the stone paving of an adjoining court. We ran forward. Frey was staggering like a drunken man as we burst into that adjoining court. Out of the mists loomed a Jotun guard, black-bearded, huge, his face a white blur in the fog.

"Who are you?" he challenged. When he saw the fair hair of my two companions, he uttered a loud cry. "Aesir!"

He struck at me with his sword, but I had the advantage of surprise. I ran in with an upward thrust of my blade, slid past his defense, ripped between the laces of his brynja. He collapsed, the alarm bubbling through the blood that filled his throat.

I began running toward the vague shape of my rocket plane, which loomed out of the mist. But suddenly I remembered that the port window had been smashed when I had first landed on the sandy beach below Midgard's frowning cliffs. Flying in the cold, thin air of the Arctic, I might lose consciousness and crash into the sea. In any case, my hands would be too numb to handle the firing wheel.

"Hold the ship against attack!" I shouted to Frey, handing him the guard's sword.

As I rushed into the cabin, I glimpsed him standing with the sword in hand, but he was swaying drunkenly. I knew he could not hold off an attack for long, and I dragged on the flying togs I had discarded before climbing to Midgard plateau. The instant I strapped the oxygen tank to my shoulders, I heard Freya's terrified scream.

"Jarl Keith, Frey is swooning, and Jotuns are coming!" I snatched a super-automatic from the supply compartment and dashed outside. The Moon slipped from behind the clouds, shining full on the Jotuns who were rushing up to attack. Horned helmet on his head, sword in hand and the golden mustache writhing above his savage lips, Loki was leading two fierce Jotun soldiers. But Freya was struggling with Frey's almost inert weight. The blade had slipped from his nerveless grasp.

"Get him into the rear of the ship and close the door!" I shouted to the woman.

The Jotun archer drew back the string of his bow to strike me down with a heavy arrow. I picked him off with a single snipe-shot. The pikeman raised his javelin, dropped it as a slug blasted away his skull. Before I could wheel on Loki and end the menace to the Aesir, Freya called to me in despair.

"Jarl Keith, I cannot get him into the ship! He has swooned."

I triggered a shot at Loki, saw him duck swiftly out of the bullet's path. Then I had no more time to fight. I hurled the gun and caught him on the right shoulder. The sword spun from his grip as he staggered back.

Frantically I ran to the cabin door and dragged Frey inside. When I pointed quickly, Freya opened the door of the freight hold while I carried him in and laid him down on the floor. I wrapped him in blankets and told Freya to do the same. It would be warmer and more easy to breathe than in the cabin, for the ship was electrically warmed and synthetically oxygenated. But the smashed window of the cabin would leak its own air and warmth, and chill and thin the air of the hold, despite the tightness of the door I closed on them as I sprang back into the pilot room.

Jotun reinforcements were charging up as I opened the jets wide and blasted off. The plane soared into the freezing air, and I was glad I had taken time to don my flying clothes and oxygen tank. Even through my wired suit, I could feel the numbing chill, and my lungs were laboring under the lessened pressure.

Far below, I saw the glimmering river through the closing mist. The tall masts of Jotun ships looked like dowels. I twisted the firing wheel to top speed, and we rose so steeply that I thought the ship would slip into a tailspin. But it righted and zoomed higher, rocketing above the misty river and the dark, fog-shrouded forests beyond. When I looked back, the ominous citadel of Jotunheim was alive with moving torches. I could well imagine the blazing anger that Loki would vent upon the Jotuns because of our escape.

"We're clear!" I thought exultantly. "Maybe by now Loki has more respect for outland science."

I set the robot controls and searched through the spare-parts compartment for a new window. Fixing the smashed port was only a few moments' work. Then I opened the oxygen nozzles wide and let the cabin fill with fresh, invigorating air and warmth. I removed my flying togs and opened the freight hold door. Freya and I helped Frey into the cabin, put him in a seat. His blurred eyes looked less helpless, and he sat unsteadily but without collapsing.

"Are you all right?" I asked anxiously.

He nodded weakly.

"Truly you outlanders have strange powers," he mumbled. "We must warn Odin of the attack . . ."

"Loki means to use those devilish storm-cones to overcome the Aesir," I said. "We've got to devise some defense against that weapon."

I went back to the controls and guided the plane above Midgard's black hills. Freya's frantic voice called to me over the roar of the rocket motor.

"Jarl Keith, Frey has fallen!"

I whipped around. He was lying on the floor, twitching. Then I saw something that horrified me. His body was covered with green spray which the Midgard snake had spat upon him. Around his bandaged wounds, his flesh was turning black!

"The venom has entered his wounds!" I cried.

I had never thought that a snake the size of Iormungandr could be poisonous. No Earthly serpent larger than nine or ten feet possesses venom. But I had forgotten that Loki's science had developed it to its huge size.

Frey opened his fluttering eyes and stared dully at us. His lips moved feebly.

"I've fought my last fight . . . The poison of the Midgard snake has slain me . . ."

"Try to fight that venom!" I urged hoarsely.

"The Norns have spun out my long life-thread at last —" he mumbled. "I would that I could see Gerda before I pass. But Wyrd ordains otherwise." His blearing eyes grew strangely brilliant and clear for an instant. "Jarl Keith, you have been a worthy comrade. I leave my kinswoman in your care, for I know you love her dearly. Try to save her in the day that approaches — the day of Ragnarok."

Freya sobbed and the Aesir's eyes dilated, as though looking past us at some gigantic, terrifying spectacle.

"I see Loki riding in fire and storm to destroy Asgard — I see the Aesir dying — I see the whole land —"

His eyes closed abruptly, and his jaw sagged as his life departed.

Freya turned a quivering, tear-stained face toward me as the plane thundered northward through the night.

"Jarl Keith, he's dead. My kinsman was so great among the Aesir and has lived so long. Now he's dead."

I felt a hard lump in my throat. Handsome, steadfast Frey had been my first friend among the Aesir.

"We cannot help him now, Freya," I said. "Damn Loki and his fiendish schemes!"

"Aye," said Freya bitterly. "My kinsman is but the first of many Aesir who must fall because the arch-traitor has been loosed."

"And that happened only because I brought the rune key into Asgard," I said in heavy self-reproach. "I have been an evil guest to the Aesir, Freya."

She clasped my hand. "Don't think thus, Jarl Keith! It is not your fault that Loki's powers brought you and the fateful rune key here. Sooner or later, he would have accomplished it somehow. All my people always feared that."

Dawn was paling in the sky. During the last half-hour we had flown over most of the length of Midgard. Against the rose-flushed sky a few miles north of us stood the high, lofty little island of Asgard, with its eyrie of gray castles amid which Valhalla loomed mountainously. Already the flying arch of Bifrost Bridge was glittering as the short polar spring night ended.

"We'll have to land on the field this side of the bridge," I mused. "There's not room enough to land safely in Asgard."

I brought the plane down safely on the bare plain of the mainland promontory. As we emerged from it, over Bifrost Bridge from Asgard a long stream of Aesir warriors came galloping. At their head rode a yellow-haired, yellow-bearded giant, his great hammer swinging.

"Thor has seen us and he comes!" Freya exclaimed.

In a few moments, Thor and the Aesir warriors reached us. The horsemen seemed awed by sight of my flying craft.

"Jarl Keith and Freya!" cried the Hammerer, his small eyes joyful as he quickly recognized us. "But where is Frey?"

"Dead," I said bitterly. "Slain in Jotunheim by the poison of the Midgard snake."

Thor looked into the plane at the dead figure, as though unable to believe his ears. He whispered blankly:

"Frey, who has ridden and sailed by my side these many centuries — dead!" Wild rage crimsoned his face and he shook the great hammer Miolnir aloft, "Loki's work! Aye, These are the first fruits of that devil's freedom!"

"Loki prepares to lead the Jotuns upon Asgard," I warned him, "Tomorrow that host of dread evil comes against us, Thor."

"Good! The sooner the better!" He turned to his Aesir warriors, who were still staring awedly at the plane. "Take the lord Frey and place him on a shield. He goes home to Asgard as a warrior should!"

Freya stood beside me, her blue eyes were bright with unshed tears as she watched them silently remove Frey's body and lay it gently upon a big shield, I put my arm around the woman comfortingly. But she did not weep now. The Viking strain was too strong in her. Though her red lips quivered, she watched steadily as the Aesir warriors lifted the shield that bore Frey's body.

We started back toward Asgard, following the warriors bearing the shield. Thor, Freya, the warriors and I walked slowly behind, leading the horses. We reached the promontory at the end of Midgard. When we started over the incredible, unrailed stone span of Bifrost Bridge, the sea was washing loud a thousand feet below us. And as we marched, the Aesir warriors behind us struck their sword-hilts against their shields in a clanging funeral rhythm.

Up the arch of the Bifrost Bridge we paced to the slow, sorrowful rhythm of that clanging. In the castle which guarded the Asgard end of the bridge, the great gates swung open for our entrance. And from the tower above the gates, we saw Heimdall blow a long, law, mournful note on the great Giallar horn.

So we passed in the brightening sunrise through the gates into Asgard, ringed round by the castles of the Aesir nobles perched upon the cliffs, dominated by the huge pile of Valhalla. Inside the gates, a hastily gathered group of the Aesir met us.

Odin was foremost. The strong, stern face of the Aesir king grew taut and strange. His eyes clouded darkly as he saw the burden upon the shield.

"So Frey had fallen to the evil of Loki and his familiars," Odin muttered. "Now I know that Wyrd stoops low over us. The Norns spin out the end of their threads for many in this land."

"Frey and I did all we could to prevent the release of Loki, lord Odin," I said. "But we failed."

"You could not succeed," Odin said broodingly. "It was written that Loki would be loosed. How soon does he come with the Jotuns against Asgard?"

"Tomorrow," I answered. "And he will be armed with his storm-cones to loose tempest and lightning on us."

"We must prepare a defense," Odin declared. "Now bear Frey's body to his castle."

CHAPTER XIV

Thor's Oath

OUR SOLEMN little procession wound across Asgard, through the streets of stone houses, past great Valhalla castle. We moved miserably toward the castle on the eastern cliffs where Frey and his line dwelt. As we approached its entrance, the lady Gerda stood waiting to meet us. The lovely face of Frey's wife went pale as she saw the stiff figure on the shield. But she did not falter.

"My lord comes home for the last time," she said quietly in the deep silence. "Bring him in."

Gerda walked beside us, her eyes fixed on Frey's dead form, as we entered the castle. We took him into the great hall of the castle, a high-roofed, big stone chamber. There the shield that bore his body was laid across wooden trestles that had been hastily procured.

I tried to speak a word of consolation to Gerda, and could not. Her strange eyes seemed not to see any of us, but remained fixed on her dead husband. She had seated herself in a chair by the body. With hands folded in her lap, she stared wordlessly. Freya plucked my arm as I stood, swaying from exhaustion. The woman's eyes were bright with tears.

"We cannot soothe her grief, Jarl Keith," she whispered. "And you are weary to the soul. You must sleep."

"Aye, sleep," boomed Thor, his heavy voice rumbling ominously. "For tomorrow we shall need every arm in Asgard."

I let thralls lead me to a small chamber in the castle. Hardly had I flung myself upon its hide bed when I was sinking into a slumber of utter physical and nervous fatigue. My dreams were troubled. Again I seemed to be facing Loki's beautiful face and the snarling wolf Fenris. Again I saw Frey confronting the venomous Midgard snake. And again, like a dim echo from far away, the dying gasp of Frey reverberated in my brain.

"I see Loki riding in fire and storm to destroy Asgard — I see the Aesir dying —"

I awoke with a shuddering start. The sun was setting. I had slept through the day. A thrall had touched my shoulder to awaken me.

"The lady Freya bade me rouse you. It is time for the lord Frey's funeral."

I hastily donned my mail coat and helmet and buckled on my sword. Then I went down to the lower floor of the castle, and looked into the hall that was now growing dusky with twilight.

Gerda still sat exactly where I had left her. Hands folded unmovingly, her lovely face was a strange, immobile mask as she looked at the body of Frey upon the shield.

Freya touched my arm. The woman had donned her own short mail tunic and helmet. Again she was the warrior-maid I had first met. Her white face was composed.

"We give Frey burial now, Jarl Keith," she said. "The shield-bearers come. You should be one of them."

Thor, dark-faced, brooding-eyed Tyr the berserk, and sad, noble-looking young Forseti had entered. We entered the hall where Gerda watched her dead.

"It is time, lady Gerda," said Thor softly.

"That is well," she said in a calm voice.

We lifted the shield that bore Frey's body. Carrying it high upon our shoulders, we paced slowly out of the castle, Freya and Gerda following.

The gloom of early dusk layover Asgard. A strong wind blew keen and cold from the northwest, wailing around the lofty cliffs. Warriors in companies of hundreds waited outside, clad in full armor. As we passed through them, they took up their place behind our cortege. They marched after us, striking their sword-hilts against their shields in that clangorous dirge.

We wound along the edge of the cliff to the stair that led down to the fiord. At the head of the stair, on the cliff-edge, were gathered Odin and his lady Frigga, old Aegir and Ran, Bragi and all the other Aesir nobles.

"Farewell, Frey," said Odin. "You have gone first into the shades, but others follow soon."

From the warriors who had followed us, from all the Aesir-folk, echoed that solemn sorrow.

"Farewell, lord Frey!"

Now we four started down the steep and narrow stair that was chiseled from the cliffside. Only Gerda and Freya followed us. The wind blew in great gusts, booming and moaning around the cliffs in the twilight. Thus we came down to the deep, narrow fiord in which floated the long dragon-ships of the Aesir. Among them, Frey's ship stood ready to give him Viking burial. It was trimmed and stacked with wood, and a low, broad wooden platform had been built amidships.

We stepped aboard and laid the shield that bore Frey's body upon that platform. Thor put Frey's sword in the dead hand. Then Frey's black horse was led into the bow of the ship. Tyr's dagger flashed, and the horse fell dead.

"Now all is ready," Thor rumbled.

We stepped back onto the shore.

"All is not yet ready," said Gerda calmly.

She stepped past up to the platform where her husband lay. When she looked down at him, her lovely face was strangely happy.

"For long," she said quietly, "my lord has lived with me at his side. He could not go on this journey into the dead without me."

Before any of us could move, she drew a dagger from her robe, and sheathed it in her heart. We watched rigidly as she fell upon the platform. Her golden hair fell across Frey's dead face.

Freya broke into wild sobbing and clung to me. We stared in horror and pity, but Thor lifted his great hammer in salute.

"Skoal to the lady Gerda!" he rumbled. "She goes proudly to death with her lord, like a true Viking."

Tyr slashed the mooring of the ship. Then he took a waiting torch from a socket, and tossed it into the resinous wood with which the ship was filled. The pile blazed up with a crackling roar, casting a red, quivering light through the deepening twilight. We bent our shoulders against the stern. The ship of death forged out on the heaving waves. Then, as the wind took its raised sail, it sprang forward like a thing alive.

Back we climbed to Asgard, my arm supporting Freya. At the top of the cliff, we stood with Odin and the other Aesir. By the light of many torches, we gazed silently at the burial ship of Frey and Gerda. Blazing red with flames, its high sail carrying it before the swift wind, the ship drove south over the heaving black waves.

"Viking funeral, for a true Viking man and his mate!" Odin declared.

Thor raised his hammer into the air. His red face was even redder by the light of the distant fire ship.

"Thy spirit hear my vow, Frey!" boomed the giant. "It was slimy Iormungandr, Loki's evil snake, that slew thee. I swear to rid Earth of that Midgard serpent in the coming battle, or die myself. Wyrd binds me to that oath!"

The blazing ship that bore the bodies of Frey and Gerda was now far away upon the dark sea. A great torch of red fire, it, was still scudding southward before the wind. Then we saw the ship's prow dip. The whole burning craft plunged down beneath the waves.

"So passes the lord Frey and his mate," said Odin's heavy voice in the silence that followed. "And now, jarls and warriors of the Aesir, we must prepare ourselves. The hosts of the Jotuns come upon the morrow, led by evil Loki, to destroy us."

"We hold Asgard safe while we live, lord Odin!" cried Bragi.

All the voices shouted chorus. I, too, joined that shout, fierce desire for vengeance on Loki and the Jotuns burning in me strongly. Only one of us did not join in that fierce yell, and that was Tyr. The berserk still stood gazing out into the windy night, his dark, brooding face unfathomable.

"Tonight we hold feast in Valhalla as ever," Odin was saying. "Now I go to prepare that which may snatch victory from Loki's grasp. Son Thor, come you with me — and you also, Jarl Keith."

The Aesir king strode with Frigga and his stalwart sons, giant Thor, Vidar and Vali, back toward the black, looming bulk of Valhalla castle. The other Aesir nobles and warriors slowly dispersed toward their own castles and homes. I remained with Freya on the edge of the cliff. The chill darkness seemed alive with voices, with winds that boomed and wailed about Asgard's cliffs as though bemoaning something to come.

Freya crept into my arms. No longer was she the fierce, proud Viking maid who had watched the burial of her kinsman and his mate. A trembling woman, she felt even as I the shadow of colossal disaster deepening with inevitable swiftness over us.

"Hold me close, Jarl Keith," she whispered. "I fear that when tomorrow night comes, we may be separated forever."

"No!" I exclaimed fiercely. "Whether living or dead, Freya, you and I shall be together."

In the darkness, her blue eyes shone up at me with bright tenderness. Her cold little hand touched my cheek.

I kissed her quivering lips. We clung together in the frigid darkness, the moaning wind wrapping around us both the dark cloak I wore over my armor.

We could hear the tramping of feet, the clanging of hammers beating out spear and arrowheads, the bustle of activity as the warships below were prepared. All the stir of preparation was for the coming battle. Freya raised her bright golden head with proud gladness.

"Come Loki and all his evil hosts, come the end of Asgard itself, and I shall not weep now," she whispered tensely. "Beloved who came to me from beyond the ice, we are one till time ends." She stepped back. "You must answer the summons of lord Odin. We meet again at the feast tonight."

My heart was throbbing with pride and gladness as I turned from her and hurried across Asgard to Valhalla castle.

CHAPTER XV

The Fire World

ODIN AND THOR were waiting for me in the great hall of Valhalla. The stern, iron-strong face of the Aesir king was heavy. As he spoke, I could hear the bustle of preparation, the clatter of shields and spears and hurrying feet throughout the great castle.

"Jarl Keith, I shall not hide from you that Asgard is in dire peril. The Jotun hosts outnumber us by many to one. Though we might repulse them, if that were all, they will be led by cunning Loki and aided by the storm-weapons of which you spoke."

I nodded wordlessly, for all this knowledge had weighed on my own mind through these last hours.

"It is necessary, unless Asgard is to perish," Odin continued, "that I devise some defense against those storm-cones. Otherwise they would blast our forces and make us easy prey."

"Can you prepare a defense against them, lord Odin?" I asked hopefully.

"I think I can," said Odin, gravely thoughtful. "I possess as much of the ancient science of our race as Loki, remember, though I have not probed into unholy researches as he did. Tell me, what did you learn of the nature of his storm-cones?"

Rapidly I told Odin and Thor what Loki himself had related to me of those amazing devices. They could project a controlled electric field to any desired spot and cause an abnormal difference of electric potential between that place and the sky. The result would be a blasting discharge of lightning.

"Ah, I understand now," Odin muttered. "Loki has found a way to draw power from the static electric charge of Earth, transform and project it in a controlled field. Truly he is a daring scientist, as always."

"Curse him and his devil's tricks!" growled Thor. "I always mistrusted him, even in the ancient days in Muspelheim."

"Couldn't there be some way of creating an electric energy field that would screen out Loki's projected field?" I asked Odin eagerly, with great anxiety.

"You have divined the only possible defense, Jarl Keith." Odin nodded. "And I could soon build a mechanism to create such a screen of energy. But it would take tremendous power to operate it. Only controlled disintegration of a large mass of intensively radioactive matter could yield such power as that."

"You said once, lord Odin, that there are tremendous masses of radioactive matter in the deep world from which the Aesir originally came."

Odin's stare narrowed.

"Are you suggesting that we could get the radioactive substances from Muspelheim?"

"That's my idea," I stated. "You told me that there was a way down into Muspelheim. It was a way by which the Aesir originally came up, and which Loki later used for his researches in the atomic fires below."

"It is true," Odin said slowly. "There is such a path down to Muspelheim, though it is a perilous and fearful one to follow. The opening to that path is in the deepest chamber of this castle. When we emerged here long ago, we built Valhalla over it. And it is the same way that Loki used to descend and tamper with the atomic fires below, until we discovered what he was doing and banished him."

"But it would be deadly dangerous for anyone to go down that way to Muspelheim and seek to bring back radioactive matter. For that deep-buried world is a place of awful, raging atomic fires. The terrific radiation is such that it streams even up through Earth's crust into this land."

"I know, but a lead garment of sufficient thickness would protect me from the radiation," I said earnestly. "I know that from my own science. Let me go on this mission, lord Odin!" He hesitated. "The lead suits which Loki used for his secret descents into Muspelheim are still here," he muttered. "It might be done, Jarl Keith. I will go with you on this perilous trip."

But Thor shook his great, shaggy head.

"No, Father, you must not go," the Hammerer declared. "You must be here to take command if Loki's forces attack before tomorrow. And you will also need all the available time to build the mechanism of which you and Jarl Keith speak." He turned to me. "I will go with Jarl Keith down into Muspelheim."

Odin reluctantly assented.

"So be it, then, though I dislike to send you, Jarl Keith, upon this fearful mission. The fight is for the sake of our people, not yours."

"The Aesir are my people, now and always, if you will let me claim that privilege!"

Odin's iron face softened, and he laid his great hand on my shoulder.

"Jarl Keith, I welcome you as one of us. Weal or woe, life or death, you are outlander no longer, but jarl and captain of the Aesir."

Hard-headed American scientist or not, I felt pride such as I had never felt before, to be accepted into the company of these mighty men.

"Now go we down to the chamber that holds the mouth of the terrible road to Muspelheim," Odin said. "Come!"

Thor and I followed out of the great hall and through corridors. We descended dark stone stairs until we reached the deepest level of Valhalla castle. We came to a door carved with runes, and with a great lock upon it. Odin touched the runes in a certain combination, and the door swung slowly inward.

By the light of the torch Thor carried, I saw that we had entered a round stone chamber of considerable size. It was dank and dusty, as though unused for ages. Standing about were dust-covered instruments and mechanisms of copper, quartz and iron, which I guessed were long unused devices of the ancient Aesir science.

In the very center of the big chamber's stone floor yawned a pit fifty feet in diameter, sinking to unguessable depths. Up from that opening beat a fierce green glow of throbbing force, from somewhere far beneath. I heard a dim, remote, roaring sound.

Most strange of all, in the opening of that pit floated a twenty-foot disk of white metal, with a squat, thick standard of metal rising from its center. It poised in the radiation, apparently without support, rocking gently as the fierce green rays from below streamed up through it.

"What in the world is that?" I asked startledly.

"That is the chariot on which you and Thor will ride down the road to deep Muspelheim," Odin explained. "And yon pit in which the disk floats is the road itself."

Odin looked somberly about the dusty room and its looming, enigmatic mechanisms.

"This is the very heart of Asgard, Jarl Keith. Up that pit-road the Aesir came long ago, fleeing from disaster-stricken Muspelheim. Over the opening of this road I caused Valhalla castle to be built. And secretly, from this chamber, Loki came and went to Muspelheim in the perilous researches that caused his exile, using the floating disk which he had devised to come and go easily."

Thor was looking in obvious dislike at the metal disk that was rocking eerily in empty air at the edge of the pit.

"I've not ridden that disk since we caught Loki in his secret researches," rumbled the bearded giant. "I've not much desire to repeat the trip, but I suppose it has to be done."

"Here are the lead suits, Jarl Keith," called Odin.

I went to the side of the chamber to which the Aesir king had gone. He had reached down, from hooks on which they hung, two of the four strange garments which had hung there, gathering dust for long. The garments were stiff robes of heavy but oddly flexible lead, falling to the ankles, with leaden boots for the feet and leaden gloves for the hands. A hood-like cowl of the same material went over the head, and had two eye-holes of heavily leaded glass for vision.

"These are the suits which Loki and the thralls he forced to help him used in the fiendish researches below," Odin said. "When Loki was forced to flee Asgard, he had to leave these behind him."

I examined the heavy garments.

"They ought to be proof against any ordinary radiation," I muttered. "But we've got to have something in which to bring back the mass of radioactive matter."

Odin nodded understandingly. "Yon crucible should serve the purpose. Put it on the disk, Thor."

The crucible was a big one of lead, and so heavy that even huge Thor grunted as he lifted it. He staggered with it to the floating disk. It rocked a little as he put the crucible on it, then quieted. Thor and I each donned one of the protective suits. The lead garments were so heavy that I felt crushed, and I could see only dimly through the dark glass of the eye-holes. Odin handed each of us a stout iron staff.

"Thor, you know from long ago how to operate the disk," he told his huge son. "While you are gone, I shall begin converting one of these mechanisms into a generator whose energy may screen us from Loki's storm-cones in the coming battle."

"We'll get the stuff to operate that generator, or not come back," I promised.

The Aesir king's iron-strong face was anxious.

"I pray the Norns that you return with it, Jarl Keith."

Thor had stepped out onto the floating disk. I followed, moving stiffly in my hampering garments, and feeling more than a little uneasy as I boarded the disk which floated in empty air.

"Crouch by the standard with me, Jarl Keith," came Thor's muffled voice. "Cling to the hand-grips."

I followed his example and crouched down beside the squat pillar which rose from the center of the disk. Upon that pillar was a single lever, movable in a graduated slot, which seemed to be the only control of the strange vehicle. There were protecting hand-grips on the pillar and across the whole disk, for passengers to cling to. Thor's lead-gloved hand clutched the lever and moved it slightly. It operated a simple mechanical device which slid open scores of tiny doors in the disk, which until now had been half — open.

At once the disk began to fall into the pit. Faster and faster we fell, the air whistling around us, and the blazing green radiation streaming violently up through the many tiny openings in the disk.

"How in the world does this thing operate?" I shouted to Thor over the roar of air. "Is it by radiation-pressure?"

I heard his muffled answer.

"You have guessed it, Jarl Keith. The metal of this disk is one that is extremely light and opaque to radiation. The pressure of the radiation from below is so terrifically powerful as to drive the disk upward. By opening the little doors and controlling the radiation through the disk, the vehicle can be poised motionless against the pressure, or caused to fall."

"Certainly Loki is a clever scientist, to have devised such a thing," I declared.

Thor growled an answer, but I could not hear, the whistling wind and din, thunderous roaring from far below were growing louder. We were falling at an appalling speed, straight down the pit. It was a ride wild beyond imagination, with the air shrieking like fiends, and the fierce green rays streaming up around us. Through every fiber of my body, even though I wore the protective lead suit, tingled stronger vibrations of the stimulating force I had felt since entering this land. It was wildly exhilarating and intoxicating.

Thor's big, lead-clothed figure crouched, his gloved hand on the control lever. His cowled head was bent as he peered tautly down through a square quartz plate in the bottom of the disk. A giddy sensation akin to nausea shook me, so swift now was our fall.

"We approach Muspelheim!" came Thor's bellow over I the roar and shriek. "Hold tightly, Jarl Keith!"

His hand moved the lever in its slot. The tiny doors in the bottom of the disk closed a little. Our fall began to slow. Pressed hard against the disk, crushed by the deceleration, I peered down through the quartz view-plate with Thor. The end of the vertical pit was close below. I saw, beneath it, a vast, fiery space.

The disk slowed further, as Thor moved the lever. Finally it hung motionless again, its weight just balanced by the pressure of radiation from below. It had halted just where the vertical pit debouched into the roof of an inconceivably vast, blazing space. An underworld of terrible atomic radiance stretched away for miles from the rock wall beside which the pit entered.

"You look upon deep Muspelheim." Thor's voice reached me

muffledly. "Once the home of the Aesir, it is the home now of the atomic fires and the creatures of the fires."

The scene before me was indescribably awe-inspiring. The vast dimensions of this mighty space beneath Earth's crust were enough to stagger the mind. This was no mere cavern, but an enormous hollow such as many have believed was left under the planet's surface by the hurling forth of the Moon.

The rocky roof was a mile above the floor. Our disk had halted just where the vertical pit entered the roof, close beside one rock wall of the great space. From the spot where Thor and I gazed, the subterranean world stretched off out of sight, to right and left and ahead.

Many miles away from us there shone a dazzling thing that dominated the whole vast, blazing fane with its brilliance. It was a colossal fountain of cold, white fire that gushed from a chasm in the floor. Hundreds of feet into the air it rose, falling back on itself in continual blinding spray. From it shot beams and banners of blinding light and force, a shaking, shuddering radiance.

All across the underworld rose similar but smaller geysers of white fire, gushing jets of radiance like that mighty distant one. Wherever the eye turned, it encountered such fiery fountains. They filled the underworld with a roaring that was deafening, and a terrific green-white radiance.

"Can your people ever have lived here?" I cried shakenly to Thor, as I gazed stupedfiedly from the floating disk.

"Aye, Jarl Keith. Centuries ago we dwelt here, where we had evolved and lived for ages. But then this was a fair world. There was no fire except that one great atomic fountain which you see far away. It was smaller then than now, yet its radiations were sufficient to keep this whole underworld warm and habitable.

"Then accursed Loki tampered with our fire fountain. He sought to stimulate it to greater activity, so that its increased radiations would make us almost immortal. He so disturbed and aroused the fountain that its fires shot up and fell here and there, all across the underworld. Eventually it set masses of radioactive matter everywhere to blazing up in atomic flame themselves.

"Thus we had to flee from disaster-smitten Muspelheim. We managed to pierce the pit up to the upper world, and clambered up it by a toilsome stair carved in its side. And since then Muspelheim has been a world of fire, forsaken by men."

I was so stunned by the awesome spectacle that I had almost forgotten our mission here. But Thor recalled it to me.

"We must not stay here long, Jarl Keith!" he warned. "The

awful radiation here would slay us if it penetrated our leaden suits."

I glanced down.

"There must be plenty of radioactive matter here, all right," I said. "But how do we get down to the floor?"

"By this stair. It's part of the ancient way by which my people escaped to the upper world."

I saw now that the disk had halted beside the landing of a stair which was chiseled from the rock wall of the underworld. The stair climbed up from the floor and disappeared into the pit-shaft by which we had descended.

Hastily, fully awakening to the peril of remaining long in this hell of fierce radiation, I helped Thor pick up the leaden crucible we had brought. We stepped from the disk to the landing, and started down the stair. It was hard walking in our stiff lead garments, and with the weight of the crucible to carry. Moreover, the stair was without any protective rail, and perilously narrow.

CHAPTER XVI

The Flame Creatures

WHEN WE reached the floor of the underworld, we stood within a hundred yards of one of the many geysers of atomic fire. Though half-blinded by its brilliance, I was able to see that it jetted from a mass of radioactive mineral whose normally slow disintegration had been tremendously accelerated. It had been kindled to this faster disintegration, I knew, by the flame that had fallen from the central fountain.

"We shall have to find a radioactive deposit unkindled as yet," I called to Thor.

He nodded his lead-cowled head vigorously.

"Let us try this direction, Jarl Keith."

We stumbled with the crucible between the geysers of atomic flame. Sometimes we were forced to go so near one of the jets that its inconceivable radiation seemed bound to penetrate our suits. Dazzled even through my lead-glass eyeholes by the raging brilliance, every fiber of my body tingling, I searched desperately for such a deposit as we required. If our suits should be penetrated, we would die horrible deaths.

"This way, Thor!" I called suddenly as I found a mass of mineral in a niche in the broken rock floor.

It was glowing with a soft light that seemed feeble in comparison with the flaming atomic fountains. I recognized it as an isotope of radium itself, never found in a natural state in my own upper world.

"There's more than enough of the stuff here, if we can dig it out!" I exclaimed. "We'll have to use our staffs."

The iron pikes we carried were ill-adapted to digging out the hard, glowing mineral. But we set to work, prying out chunks of the stuff and tossing them into the crucible. As I straightened once, panting for breath, I glimpsed an amazing sight in the middle distance.

Around one of the geysers were circling and flitting a dozen things that looked like swirling spheres of flame, with coiling, brilliant tentacles of light.

"Those things look as though they were alive!" I yelled in horror.

Thor straightened to see.

"Flame-children!" he exclaimed, his muffled voice suddenly

anxious. He turned to me hastily. "They are alive, in a way. But it is not life like ours. They are creatures evolved somehow from the flaming radiation of this underworld of atomic fires. We believe they consist of force currents that cohere in a permanent pattern, which possess powers of movement and perhaps dim intelligence. We don't know much about them, for they've evolved here since the Aesir left poor Muspelheim."

"They look beautiful, like flame-winged birds of light," I said, staring in awe and fascination.

"They're dangerous, Jarl Keith — pure concentrated atomic energy!" warned the Hammerer. "We must be gone before they find us."

I redoubled my toil of helping to dig out the radioactive chunks. We had the crucible half-full of the precious mineral when I felt a terrific shock of force against my back. I whirled around, uttered a cry. One of the dazzling flame-children was poised behind me, had just touched my suit. The mere touch of the weird creature had burned almost through the thick lead!

"We've got to get out!" Thor bellowed. "The thing has almost pierced your suit. The radiation will penetrate it in a few minutes, and you'll die horribly."

"But we haven't all the radioactive matter that Odin will need," I protested.

"We have most of it. If you perish here, we'll never get even this much back to him. Quick, up the stair to the disk!"

He grabbed the crucible's handle. Reluctantly I took the other handle and started with him toward the stair. As we hastened with our heavy load between the roaring geysers of atomic fire, I looked back. The one of the flame-children that had touched me experimentally was now joining several other dazzling creatures like itself, and drifting after us.

Hastily we started up the stair. With some relief, I saw that the flame-children did not follow us, but drifted on and started circling and flitting around another of the fire fountains. Apparently the dim intelligence of the creatures, if indeed they possessed any, had lost interest in us.

Panting and exhausted, we reached the landing and set the crucible down on the floating disk. Thor hastily adjusted the controls to make up for the increased weight on it. As he crouched down, preparatory to starting up the shaft, I noticed something.

"Thor, what is that door up there, high in the roof?" He turned his gaze to follow my pointing finger. The door looked like a massive sliding sheet of dull metal, set in the roof of the underworld some distance from us. There was a shielded mechanism of some kind set in the rock by the door, obviously controlling it.

"That is the forbidden research upon which Loki was engaged, and which caused us to banish him from Asgard," Thor explained. "Above that door is a tunnel connected with the sea of the upper world. If the door were opened, sea water would rush down into this underworld."

"Good lord!" I cried in horror. "If sea water ever poured down into this world of fire, there'd be an explosion that would shake the planet!"

"Aye, and Odin saw that danger," Thor said. "Loki planned to admit only enough sea water to produce the titanic power of which he had need in his experiments. But Odin pointed out that if anything went wrong — if this door were completely opened and the sea rushed down unchecked into Muspelheim — there would be such an explosion as would rend the whole land above. It was the reason for Loki's banishment."

As Thor spoke, he was moving the control lever. The floating disk began to rise in the vertical shaft, out of the fiery underworld. With all the tiny valve-doors closed, it rose quickly under the pressure of the powerful radiation. We shot up the dark shaft at a speed that almost equaled that of our descent.

We were none too soon. A savage pain in my back told me that the radiation had just been starting to penetrate my weakened protective garment. Already it had scorched my flesh!

Clinging to the rocking, rising disk, I held the crucible to keep it from sliding away. The radioactive matter in it shed a feeble glow upon the dark walls of the pit as they raced downward. Then Thor slowed our rise, and finally the disk came to a halt at the mouth of the shaft. Again we were in the torchlit chamber under Valhalla castle.

Odin was awaiting us. The Aesir uttered an exclamation of relief as Thor and I stumbled off the disk with the crucible and removed our stiff garments.

"Lord Odin, I fear we didn't get all the radioactive fuel you'll need for your mechanism," I said bitterly. "It was my fault that we were forced to leave —"

Odin looked with a shadow of worry in his eye at the half-filled crucible. But he spoke confidently to me.

"It should be enough, Jarl Keith, to defend us from Loki's storm weapons. See, I have converted another mechanism into such a generator as we will need for that defense."

The mechanism was concealed by a spherical copper cover

upon which was mounted a smaller copper ball. There was a hopper in its side, into which we poured the chunks of glowing mineral.

"It should have power enough to maintain a defensive screen against the force of Loki's storm-cones for a short time," Odin said. "If he should use the storm-cones for longer than that —"

He did not finish, but I shared the deep worry that was etched in his strong face.

"I saw Loki's handiwork below," I said, and described the sliding door in the roof of the fire-world, which Loki had designed to admit sea water. "No wonder you cast Loki out for such a terrifically dangerous plan."

"Aye, it was Baldur who discovered that plan, and was slain by Loki for exposing it," Odin said somberly. "Loki had perfected a remote control for that sliding door, operating by tuned vibration. Here it is."

And Odin showed me, among the many dust-covered instruments in the chamber, a small, square silver box. On it was mounted a knob whose pointer could be turned along a semi-circular scale.

"Turning this knob would open the sea-door a bit or wide," the Aesir king said. "When Loki fled from Asgard, he took this control box with him. And when we trapped him in that cave below Midgard, and we were about to kill him, Loki threatened to open the sea-gate wide and destroy us all. That was why we had to agree not to kill him, if he would surrender this control box to us. He did surrender it. We kept our word and did not kill him, but placed him in the suspended animation in which he lay for so long."

Odin went to the door and called up through the corridors for some of his thralls to come. When they came, he bade them carry out the big spherical copper generator.

"We shall place it on Vigrid field, on the mainland across Bifrost Bridge," he said, "and keep it under guard tonight. For it is there that we must make our stand against Loki's forces when they come in all their fury."

He, Thor and I followed the thralls as they bore the heavy mechanism through Valhalla castle and out into the windy, gusty night. Torch-bearing thralls went ahead to illuminate the way. Lights shone from all the castles of Asgard. The Moon was hidden by driving clouds as we moved in a little torchlit group across the giddy span of Bifrost to the flat field on the opposite promontory.

My plane was still where I had landed it. Aesir warriors and mounted scouts were on guard, watching toward the south for the first approach Of Loki and the Jotun horde. As Odin directed the placing of the copper mechanism, I went to my plane. Something had occurred to me which might enable me to devise an additional weapon for the coming battle.

In the plane were the half-dozen big signal rockets which were to be used in case I made a forced landing and had to summon help. I began taking the rockets apart, pouring out the gun powder in them, and carefully unfixing the detonators. At the end of a half-hour, I had made three crude hand-grenades or small bombs. I hoped they might be of some use against the Jotuns, who knew nothing of explosives. I left the bombs in the plane and emerged to find Thor waiting for me.

"My father has already returned to Asgard," the Hammerer told me. "And it is time we followed him, for our nightly Valhalla feast begins soon."

"Thor, what of tomorrow's battle?" I asked. "If it comes to sword and spear, with the Jotuns outnumbering us many times, what can we do?"

"We can triumph or we can die!" boomed the giant. "And if it is death — well, the Aesir have lived long and are not afraid to die, so long as we take our enemies with us." He tossed his great hammer in the air and caught it in outstretched hand, as though it were a willow wand. "Be not impatient, Miolnir. You'll not thirst long. And now to Valhalla, Jarl Keith."

Valhalla was blazing with torchlight when we entered it. Logs in the great hearth burned high. In the flickering torchlight, all the captains and great warriors of the Aesir were gathered at the many tables. The Aesir nobles were appearing, striding toward the high table on the dais. I took my place beside Freya. Beyond her were the two empty seats of Frey and Gerda, then Bragi and Idun, old Aegir and his wife, and brooding, silent Tyr.

Odin and Frigga entered, and we all stood up. The Aesir king's eye surveyed us with stern pride.

"Be seated, jarls and captains," he boomed. "Let us eat and drink as of old. Though war and death surge upon us tomorrow, yet is there no fear in our hearts."

"Skoal to Odin!" rang Forseti's deep voice.

We seized our drinking-horns and raised them high to a crashing shout of confidence and pride.

"Skoal to the king!"

We drained the mead and sat down. The tall serving-maidens hastened to bring us more drink and meat. The din of voices and laughter rang forth, loud as ever. The deepening shadow of dire disaster which lay over Asgard that night intensified, rather than lessened, the merriment of the feast. Horn after horn of the sweet, potent mead we drank.

Beside me, Freya's blue eyes clung to my face. The shadowed tenderness and love in them was more heart-stirring to me than all else.

"Come good or ill, Freya," I whispered, "it is worth having lived to sit here tonight with you and your people."

"Aye, Jarl Keith," she replied. But there was wistfulness in her voice as she added: "I would that I could foretell our sitting here again tomorrow."

Suddenly all the cheery voices died. Into the hall strode tall Heimdall, warder of Asgard's gates.

"Why are you here, Heimdall?" Odin asked. "Is it not your task tonight to watch over Bifrost Bridge, and sound the great blast on Giallar horn when the enemy approaches?"

"Lord Odin, Loki has sent a herald to us," Heimdall answered. "That herald, the Jotun king Utgar, I have admitted under truce. He waits to enter."

Fierce passion leaped into every face as the men reached for their weapons. Thor raised his great hammer menacingly, but Odin spoke with stern calm.

"Let the herald of Loki enter."

Utgar came alone into Valhalla's blazing torchlight. Yet the big, black-bearded Jotun king came swaggering, bearing himself like a conqueror as he strode up to our table where the nobles of the Aesir sat.

CHAPTER XVII

Magic Science

UTGAR'S BRUTAL face showed no sign of fear as he met the fiery gaze of his deadly enemies. He spoke to Odin, his coarse, rasping voice loud with utter confidence.

"I bring a message from the lord Loki, ruler of Midgard and soon to be ruler of Asgard."

A fierce exclamation went up from every throat. But Odin's stern face did not change as he replied.

"Speak Loki's message."

"These are the words of Loki," Utgar said loudly. "'Odin and the other Aesir, the time of your downfall has come. I, whom you cast out long ago, whom you prisoned for centuries, am now free and thirsty for vengeance. Tomorrow I come against you with the Jotuns. We shall have three warriors for each warrior of yours, three ships for each of your ships. You cannot stand against us.

"'But because I was once of your blood, I shall offer you your lives. If you swear to submit to me as your ruler, if you become my subjects as the Jotuns are and crown me your king in Valhalla hall, then shall you retain your lives. Think well before you refuse this offer. If you refuse it, I shall utterly destroy you all.' These are the words of Loki. What answer, lord Odin?"

"I'll answer now with Miolnir!" Thor roared, rising with crimson rage on his face.

A fierce chorus of yells from every throat there, including my own, seconded his cry. But Odin waved us to silence. He spoke slowly, solemnly, gazing gravely down at Utgar.

"Take this answer to Loki, Jotun. Tell him that he knows well the Aesir will never yield to his demands. We will fight until our swords break in our hands, until our hands be shorn away, until our breath is no more in us. But we will not take back among us the murderer Loki who long ago proved traitor to our race.

"And tell Loki this also. Tell him that he shall never — even though he and his Jotun hosts utterly overcome us — reap profit from his work. For I say that before that shall happen, all this land will quail beneath destruction. Flame and death shall eat up Midgard and Asgard alike, and all the Jotuns and the Aesir. Tell the arch-traitor that!"

Involuntarily Utgar recoiled from the dark, dreadful menace in

Odin's voice. Then the Jotun king drew his huge figure scornfully erect.

"Think not that our lord will be frightened by such words," he retorted. "You have asked for doom, and doom you shall have."

He turned to go, but Tyr, the brooding berserk, stepped in front of him.

"You know me, Utgar," said Tyr in a slow, bitter voice. "Look for me in tomorrow's battle. I will look for you."

"Come and find me, then, Aesir," laughed Utgar savagely. "Too long have I heard of your valor. Tomorrow I'll test it with my sword."

Utgar strode proudly out of the hall, Heimdall following. In the silence, we heard the Jotun king gallop across Asgard to Bifrost Bridge.

"Let the feast go on," bade Odin at last. Drinking commenced again, the fierce babble of voices arising. My head spun from the mead that I had drunk as the hours went by. Freya sat silent, close inside the circle of my arm, looking up ever and again at my face. I saw Odin brooding as he watched his people make merry on the brink of dreadful war. Pride in these Aesir, gratitude that they allowed me to be one of them, filled me.

The first light of dawn began slanting through the windows. Bragi stepped forward with his harp, and all voices died as the gentle-faced skald touched the quivering strings. His clear voice rang martial-loud through Valhalla.

> *Now comes the great hour*
> *When Norn-spinners gather*
> *The fate-threads of warriors*
> *Of Aesir and Jotun.*
> *Now Wyrd's dark daughters*
> *Make ready the battle,*
> *The struggle long fated*
> *'Twixt darkness and light.*

Bragi sang on, firing the blood with the stirring strains. And when he had finished, a tremendous shout of applause roared from us all. As the echoes of our shout died, there came on their heels from far away the low, long reverberation of a horn-blast.

Louder and louder it grew as we listened in tense silence, waxing until the deep, tremendous note of that mighty trumpet throbbed through every corner of Asgard. Then it fell and died away.

"The great blast of Giallar horn," Odin said with quiet sternness. "Heimdall warns that the hosts of Loki approach."

We sprang to our feet. Odin's voice rang in quick command.

"We go forth to meet them. On the field Vigrid, on the other side of Bifrost Bridge, we will await them. Gather your men and horses. Aegir, you and Niord command our fleet! Put out with all our ships and lie off Asgard until you see along which coast the Jotun fleet comes."

With a yell the Aesir nobles and captains poured out of Valhalla. Trumpets blared out in the dawn, and there was the thunder of galloping horses, the clanking tramp of marching men hurrying up, the roar of orders shouted loudly. I remained in the almost empty hall with Freya, Odin and his family. The Aesir king was putting over his mail brynja a silver emblem carved with runes.

Vidar, the tall second son, brought Odin's great sword, and the king buckled it on. Thor, his little eyes blazing with battle-light, was swinging great Miolnir in the air, giving a last test to the strength of its helve.

Odin looked into the beautiful face of the lady Frigga.

"Farewell, my wife," he said in his deep voice. "We come back victors or dead men, as Wyrd wills it."

I had taken Freya into my arms. Almost fiercely I held her bright head between my hands and kissed her. Bright sunbeams from a window lit her hair to dazzling gold as I released her. Her blue eyes looked up into mine without a shadow of fear in their proud depths.

"Jarl Keith, I must remain with the women instead of riding by your side as I would wish. But my heart goes with you. I am proud that you from the outlands fight today beside my people."

"Your people are mine, Freya," I answered. "It was I who brought the key that loosed Loki. I can only atone for that by fighting against the devil today."

Odin was striding toward the exit of the great hall. I tore myself from Freya and followed with giant Thor, Vidal and Vali. We emerged from Valhalla castle into the bright day. Before us were massed the warriors of Asgard, helmets and mail gleaming in the Sun. Three thousand horsemen and five thousand footmen they numbered, their jarls and captains sitting their horses at the head of the men.

A great shout greeted Odin as we emerged. Thralls held our horses as we swung into the saddles. Thor vaulted heavily onto his great black stallion. Odin raised his hand high and shouted ringingly:

"To Vigrid!"

We spurred forward, the king, his sons and I galloping at the head of the massed horsemen. Across the city Asgard we rode, toward the castled gates of Bifrost. They swung open as we approached, and Heimdall, warder of the gates, was waiting for us on his own steed.

The guards on the tower above again sounded the great, throbbing blast of Giallar horn as we rode through the gates and onto the bridge. With Odin leading us, our horsemen streaming out in narrow file with armor shining gold in the dazzling Sun, we galloped up the arch of the rainbow bridge. Like thunder clattered our horses' hoofs on that flying arc of stone.

Far below us raged the green sea between Asgard and Midgard. Far back to our right, from the eastern cliffs of Asgard, the Aesir ships were putting out to sea under Aegir's command. Forty big dragons of war, square sails raised to the wind, brazen beaks dipping into the heaving waves, they quickly moved out to await the coming of the Jotun fleet.

Wild exultation was throbbing in me like wine as we rode down the descending arch of Bifrost Bridge. I had forgotten that I was Keith Masters of the outside world. I had forgotten everything except that I was one of the Aesir, that I was to fight beside them for Freya and for Asgard against the savage hosts of evil Loki.

We halted on the open, rocky plain that lay at the northern extremity of Midgard. Behind us arched the rainbow bridge leading to Asgard. In front of us, beyond the flat field Vigrid, extended the dark, forested hills of Midgard. Odin had halted us beyond the hillock upon which his spherical copper generator stood, and near which my plane was parked.

"The footmen will mass in our center under Vidar," Odin ordered. "Half our horsemen on the left wing under Thor, and half on the right under Heimdall."

By now the infantry was streaming across Bifrost Bridge in dense, long files, archers, and spearmen, and swordsmen. Thor bellowed the orders that drew them and the horsemen up in front of the little hillock. Odin had dismounted and climbed the hillock to his generator, and I followed him. Finally Thor, having completed the disposition of our forces, rode up the hillock to where the Aesir king and I were examining the generator.

"They come!" boomed Thor, pointing southward with his gleaming hammer.

We peered intently through the bright daylight. From the south, the glitter of a forest of helmets and spear-points flashed in the Sun as a dense mass of Jotun soldiery advanced along the cliff-edge, screened by horsemen. Far out on the sea to the right, a great fleet of dragon-ships was sailing northward. There were at least a hundred of the black Jotun long-ships, and the Aesir vessels were advancing to meet them. In the south, a growing darkness was clouding the heavens. A strange dusk was creeping up rapidly across the brilliant sky.

"Loki's storm-cones!" I shouted. "See where he has set them up on that crest, lord Odin!"

I pointed. Southward, well behind the advancing Jotun army, rose a crest. Upon it was a small group of clustered objects that gleamed in the last rays of the half-obscured Sun.

"Aye, I see," Odin said in his deep voice. "Loki prepares to loose his lightnings upon us, as we feared."

The Aesir king began to manipulate the enigmatic controls of his big spherical generator, to throw up a defensive screen. The wind was moaning around us with increasing force as the darkness spread rapidly across the sky. The gloom seemed to boil up visibly from the distant crest where Loki had his storm-cones, and from which he was spraying a terrific electric field to unlock the tempest.

Down in the sea beyond the cliffs, the dark waves were churning ever higher. They and the shrieking winds were wildly tossing the Jotun and Aesir ships that maneuvered swiftly for battle.

Crash! Out of the night-black sky, a blazing flash of white lightning had struck amid our massed footmen. It left a heap of scorched dead. On its heels came another blinding bolt that blasted three horsemen.

"Lord Odin, Loki's lightnings begin to slay my men!" roared Heimdall from the right wing. "Let us charge them!"

"Wait!" Odin called, undismayed.

At the same time, the spherical copper generator began to throb with power. The radioactive matter in it, which Thor and I had procured with such risk from deep Muspelheim, was breaking down into pure power. The energy was being transformed into a radiant shell of power that was broadcast from the smaller copper ball atop the generator.

Up into the storm-nighted sky, Odin's mechanism flung a great halo of glowing light. The halo that tented our forces stopped the blazing lightning-bolts that had begun to decimate us! Those blinding flashes hit the halo and splashed harmlessly upon it.

"It shields us from Loki's storm-cones!" I cried jubilantly. "We've neutralized his best weapon!"

"Wait, Jarl Keith, before you exult," warned Odin. "There is not enough radioactive fuel to operate this mechanism much longer. When it stops, Loki's lightnings will play yet greater havoc with us."

"Can't we charge with all our horsemen and destroy Loki and his devilish weapons?" Thor cried fiercely.

"As soon as we leave the defense of this generator's screen of energy, Loki's lightnings will cleave us," Odin replied.

I realized the desperate nature of the emergency. If the Aesir and the Jotuns were to fight this battle on anything like even terms, Loki's storm-cones must be destroyed! Even if they were, the Aesir would be facing overwhelming numbers. But there would be a chance for victory, at least, whereas there would be no chance at all if Loki's forces were not checked.

In this emergency, my eyes fell on my plane parked some distance to the rear of our forces. Suddenly I remembered the bombs I had made the night before, for possible use in the battle.

"Lord Odin, I think that I may be able to destroy Loki's weapons!" I cried eagerly. "In my flying craft I have a weapon of the kind my people use in war. Let me try it."

"Can any flying ship live in this tempest?" the Aesir king asked incredulously.

I wondered, too. The storm that raged over this strange battlefield had now become chaotic in its insensate fury. From all the black sky over us, bolts of lightning induced by Loki's storm-cones were sizzling and flashing down. Though they were splattering on Odin's defense screen, the mounts of our horsemen were rearing wildly. Our warriors were white-faced in the light of the flashes. In the south, the mighty Jotun army was forming up to advance against us.

"I can make it!" I persisted without conviction. "I'll circle back around the worst of this storm."

"Then go, Jarl Keith, and the Norns guide you," Odin said reverently.

CHAPTER XVIII

The Battle for Asgard

I RACED back toward the plane. In a moment I had the rocket motor roaring, and then I managed a perilous take-off from the field. Raging winds, blowing now in this direction and now in that, threatened to hurl my rising plane back to the field. Sheets and flares of blinding lightning dazzled my eyes. But I rose and zoomed out over the sea, to circle back and approach Loki's position from the rear.

I hurtled through the unnatural darkness over the water. Lightning flares gave me a momentary glimpse of Aesir and Jotun ships locked in death-combat down on the wild waters. I rocketed over them. Then I swung back toward the cliffs of Midgard and came roaring down from behind upon the crest where Loki had his storm-cones.

I had the cabin-window open, and my crude bombs near at hand. As I dived steeply, I peered down at the crest. Loki stood by the vicious storm-cones. The big mechanisms were clustered close together, their quartz nozzles pointed toward the distant Aesir forces. A fine violet electrical brush played over them as they sprayed their controlled static field.

I saw Loki's startled white face, and the alarmed features of Utgar, Hel and the Jotun captains as my plane swooped down. Diving within a few yards of the storm-cones, I dropped four small bombs. There was a crimson flare in the lightning-seared blackness behind me. I looked back to see the storm-cones, all but one, lying shattered and dismounted. I glimpsed Loki and Utgar. Unharmed, the Aesir arch-traitor was shouting orders as the Jotuns ran to their horses.

"Score one for my science," I muttered between my teeth, as I hurled the plane back toward the Aesir positions.

The single remaining storm-cone was still operating, and lightning was flaring and thunder rolled. But the terrific hail of bolts that had threatened to destroy the Aesir had stopped.

"Well done, Jarl Keith!" roared Thor, when I had landed my plane and run back to the hillock where Odin and his captains stood.

"It was well done," Odin declared. "For my generator is faltering now. Had you not destroyed the storm-cones, we would have been helpless."

"Loki's preparing to advance with all the Jotun forces," I said breathlessly. "See, there they come now!"

The Jotuns were deploying on the farther side of Vigrid field. At least ten thousand unmounted warriors formed up behind their wide screen of cavalry.

"There rides the arch-traitor!" cried Heimdall wrathfully.

I saw Loki. He rode behind the cavalry, at the head of the massed Jotun footmen. His bright golden helmet gleamed in the lightning flashes, his white steed curveting. Besides Loki's horse ran a great, gray shape — the huge wolf, Fenris, coming like a war-dog with its master into battle.

"If only Iormungandr were with him, too!" rasped Thor. "The Midgard snake must die this day, to fulfill my oath."

The archers of the Jotuns, advancing behind their screen of horsemen, were discharging their missiles. Arrows rattled down like rain among us. Men dropped from their mounts and horses squealed with pain.

"Take your places, but do not charge till I give the word," Odin ordered.

"Are we to be riddled without striking back a blow?" cried Thor furiously.

"Wait till I give the signal," Odin bade sternly. "Both our wings of horsemen shall ride at the center and split through their main body. Vidar will follow with our footmen. Then, if Wyrd wills it, we shall cut their split forces to bits."

Odin rode forward, and I followed with Vali, Bragi, Forseti, and the other of the Aesir captains. Taking up our position between Thor's horsemen on the left and Heimdall's on the right, we waited. I felt the awful suspense of the moment. The arrows rattled down among us during the slow advance of the great Jotun host. The thunder and lightning of the storm still grumbled across the dark sky. In the face of them all, the horsemen and footmen of the Aesir waited silently and motionlessly behind Odin.

The Jotuns were well within bowshot, and their arrows were taking even greater toll. So close were they that back among them I could make out the white face of Loki, urging them forward. I could see big Utgar, the Jotun king, riding beside the arch-traitor. An ancient feud was rushing toward its climax in these last moments. I felt the tension of men who were somehow more than men. When this battle joined, it would be the clash of cosmic forces . . .

"Now!" cried Odin, raising his mailed fist and flashed his sword high.

The trumpets of the Aesir blared wildly in answer. With a yell of pent-up tenseness, we spurred our horses and galloped forward. Our two mounted wings converged, charging right at the center of the great Jotun army. Riding forward with the others, I was scarcely conscious of individual action. Instinctively I spurred and drew my sword and leaned forward over my saddle-bow.

Before me, Odin's mighty figure galloped with great sword still raised high. Beside me, Thor was already whirling his gigantic hammer, bellowing his terrifying battle-cry. Beyond him were Heimdall, Forseti and Bragi. And behind us thundered the three thousand Aesir horsemen, followed by the footmen under Vidar, Vali and Tyr.

Arrows showered among us. Men and horses tumbled, crashing in our midst as we galloped in that wild charge. Thunder roared deafeningly from the blackened sky ahead to drown our yelling trumpets. Lightning flashed blindingly across the sky.

We struck the screen of the Jotun horsemen like a thunderbolt, tore through them as a sword tears through paper. Then our charge carried us smashing deep into the main body of the Jotun army. All Earth must have felt the splintering shock of that collision! My horse stumbled over Jotun bodies. I leaned from the saddle and struck furiously with my sword at black-bearded warriors who sought to reach me with ax and blade. I hewed down two enemies before their spears could touch my side.

All around me, swords were banging on helmets, men yelling in fierce blood-lust or shrill death agony, hamstrung horses squealing horribly, shields crashing together with deafening clangor. The trumpets of the Aesir were blaring unceasingly. The hoarse horns of the Jotuns roared a savage answer.

Thor, close beside me in the battle, was forcing his stallion forward. His huge hammer kept falling like a thing endowed with its own life upon the helmets of the Jotuns. Miolnir's steel was red with blood and gray with brains as the bearded, red-faced giant whirled it. Thrice in as many moments, he beat down Jotuns who would have slain me. And on my other side, Heimdall was wielding an ax like a woodsman, and Vidar was riding forward through the corpses he had made.

Right in front of us, Odin's eagle helmet gleamed through the chaos of battle. The great sword rose and fell as the Aesir king forced deeper into the Jotun host.

"For Asgard!" rang his deep voice.

And from the Aesir horsemen and footmen behind us shouted an answering chorus.

"Follow the king! Strike for Asgard!"

The Jotun host began to split and give way before our concentrated assault. Though they greatly outnumbered us, we were driving a wedge between them.

"They waver!" shouted Vidar, wildly exultant. "Push hard and the battle is ours. They are breaking!"

As we forced forward, the Jotun footmen were giving ever more rapidly. If we could split them in two, cut them up and destroy them —

"Loki comes!" screamed Heimdall.

I saw his golden helmet shining through the murk of lightning-seared storm. Loki was pushing fearlessly through the Jotun host toward us. His face was white and beautiful with the exhilaration of battle as he came through the fight toward us. Beside him rode Utgar, and between them ran the great, gray shape of Fenris.

"Stand firm, Jotuns!" Utgar was yelling to his wavering host. "The lord Loki is with us!"

With a fierce war-cry, Odin spurred forward to meet Loki. Thor, Vidar, Heimdall, Bragi and I were all close behind the Aesir king. Heimdall and Bragi, forcing farther ahead, met the charge of Loki and Utgar first. I saw Loki's sword flash and Heimdall tumbled from his horse, stabbed through.

Utgar's ax had crashed down upon Bragi's helm at the same moment. From Thor came an awful yell of wrath as he saw our two comrades fall.

"Come to meet me, traitor!" he bellowed to Loki.

But Odin reached the arch-demon instead. Beneath the flare of lightning, they struck at each other with swords that flashed like streaks of light. Fearless, blazing and beautiful shone Loki's face as he fought. His silver voice pealed in exultation.

"At last, Odin, I repay you for my long imprisonment!"

But Odin, at that moment, struck forth fiercely with all his strength in a great blow at Loki's helm. Loki swerved, but the sword grazed his helmet. The stunning force of the blow sent him heeling back in his saddle.

"Death for Loki!" yelled the Aesir behind us in wild triumph.

A snarling, terrible roar, a scream of warning from my lips, both broke at the same moment. The giant wolf Fenris, as Loki was stricken aback by that terrible blow, leaped up like a gray thunderbolt at Odin. His huge jaws closed upon Odin's throat. Holding fast, he dragged the Aesir king from the saddle.

"Odin falls!" raged the shout of joy from the Jotun host.

I had already leaped from my saddle. I struck a terrific blow at Fenris as the huge wolf tore at Odin's prostrate body. My sword slashed deep into the wolf's shoulder. He turned, his green eyes blazing hell-fires, and catapulted at me.

But with a hoarse shout, Vidar struck at the charging wolf with his ax. The blow severed Fenris' head from his shoulders in one tremendous stroke. Odin's throat was torn into red ribbons. His eyes were closed and he seemed barely living as Thor lifted him.

"Odin is slain!" pealed Loki's silver voice. "Now falls Asgard. On, Jotuns!"

Loki had recovered from the stunning slash that had been Odin's last. He was urging the Jotuns forward, his eyes flaring with unhuman rage at the slaying of his wolf. The Aesir charge had halted, our warriors dismayed by the fall of Odin. And now, as the Jotuns rushed forward on us, we were pushed back by their superior numbers.

Back toward the end of the field, the cliff-edge from which Bifrost Bridge sprang, we were forced. Though the Aesir fought like madmen, they were falling in ever-increasing numbers before the yelling hosts of Jotuns. Thor had taken Odin's body and was bearing it back with us as we retreated. From all sides except the rear, the Jotuns surged upon us. The slaughter here was terrific. I seemed to be fighting in an unreal dream.

There was no standing against the heavier Jotun mass. Our shattered forces streamed over the high arch of Bifrost Bridge, through the gates of Asgard. Vidar, Tyr, Forseti and I came last.

Now all our surviving forces were safe within the gates. Utgar and Loki were leading the Jotuns hastily up onto the bridge after us. But as the winches inside the guard-castle creaked hastily, the gates were slowly swinging shut. Loki yelled an order. As though obeying a prepared plan, a score of Jotuns flung heavy spears into the hinges of the closing gates. The spears jammed the hinges, and the gates stopped closing.

"Push shut the gates!" Vidar yelled to the men at the winches.

"We cannot, for they are jammed!" was the frantic answer.

Across the rainbow bridge, Loki was leading his men forward and crying to them triumphantly.

"Forward, Jotuns! Over the bridge! The gates of Asgard are open to us!"

CHAPTER XIX

Swords Athirst

VIDAR YELLED to the warriors behind us.

"Clear the hinges, some of you! The rest of us will hold back the Jotuns!"

He sprang out onto Bifrost Bridge. Tyr, Forseti and I, with a score of Aesir warriors, leaped after him. The men behind us worked frantically to pull out the heavy spears that had jammed the hinges of Asgard's gates. We four stood abreast on the arched bridge, our warriors behind us, facing the Jotun masses as they rushed up behind Loki and Utgar.

The storm darkened the whole sky, and wild winds threatened to sweep us from the unrailed, narrow span on which we stood. Lightning flared continually across the sinister sky, and the thunder was rolling louder.

Tyr had torn off his brynja and thrown away his helmet. His great breast bare, streaked with blood, he held two swords in his hands. His cavernous eyes glared with a terrible light as he stepped in front of us. He yelled in a howl like that of a wild beast to the advancing Jotuns.

"Berserk am I! Who comes against me?"

The Jotuns pushing up onto the narrow bridge hesitated at sight of him, for he was truly terrible in his berserk madness.

"I await you, Utgar!" Tyr howled, his body quivering. "Come, for these swords are athirst!"

Utgar answered with a roar of rage. He and Loki, dismounted now, came up the arch of the bridge against us at the head of the Jotun mass. Tyr did not wait their coming. With a ferocious scream, our berserk companion sprang to meet them.

His two swords leaped like living things. Utgar's ax shore into his side — and Tyr laughed! Shouting with glee, he smote Utgar's head from his shoulders with a single awful stroke. Five Jotuns fell before him as he raged in berserk fury. Abruptly Loki's blade stabbed through his heart. Tyr swayed, staggered at the edge of the bridge. Then he crumpled and fell clear from the stone, plummeting down toward the raging, stormy sea far below.

Vidar, Forseti and I had been rushing forward with our men to support Tyr. Now we met the Jotuns, who were maddened by the killing of Utgar, urged on by Loki's silver voice.

For whole minutes we held the bridge against them! How, I do not know. Before my eyes was only a blur of flashing steel and wolfish faces, into which I struck by instinct rather than by design. I felt the red-hot stabs of sword-blades in my left shoulder and right thigh; I saw Forseti reel back, dying from one of Loki's incredibly swift, deadly thrusts. I glimpsed the arch-fiend's wrathful, beautiful face as he fought with Vidar.

We were pushed back over the arch of the bridge, toward the gates. A yell crashed up from the men behind us.

"The gates are freed!"

We staggered back through the small opening of the nearly closed gates. Instantly the gates were slammed shut in the faces of Loki and his hordes. For several moments we stood motionless, panting, wild-eyed, covered with blood. The Jotun hordes were banging vainly at the gates with sword and ax.

No more than a few hundred Aesir warriors remained as exhausted, wounded survivors of that dreadful battle. Out on Vigrid field, the dead lay in thousands. Ravens were swooping down on the pathetic corpses from the storm-black sky.

"Get to the towers and use your bows upon Loki's horde!" Vidar called hoarsely to part of our warriors.

They obeyed, and arrows began to rain down on the besiegers on the bridge. The howling of the Jotuns was loud even through the deepening thunder of the storm, as they sought to batter down the gates, yet avoid their own slaughter.

Vidar hastened with us through the guard-castle to the stone plaza beyond. There Odin lay upon the stones. Thor was kneeling beside his dying father. Odin's lips stirred, his wavering stare held a feeble, dying light as he looked up at his giant son.

"The Norns sever my thread," he whispered "Doom falls upon me, as Wyrd ordains — upon Asgard, too, I fear. If Loki prevails, you must do that which I ordered you."

"I will, Father," rumbled Thor, his big hand clenching tight the helve of his mighty hammer. "But stay with us!"

Odin's life was already gone, though, spent by his last effort to speak.

"Bear him to Valhalla!" ordered Thor's great voice as he arose.

"Loki and some of the Jotuns move away," called a warrior from the guard-castle tower.

We hurried back and looked through the loopholes in the gates. Loki and half the Jotun forces were striding back across the bridge and Vigrid field, marching southward. The rest of the Jotuns still battered at the gates, heedless of the arrows that fell upon them from above.

"Loki plans some trick," Thor muttered.

"Where are our ships?" Vidar cried. "Look!"

He pointed down at the sea east of Asgard. There the waves were running high and foam-white beneath the howling winds of the storm. I saw the Jotun fleet below, hacked and reduced to less than forty almost useless ships. But they were beating southward along the coast, parallel to Loki's marching force. Scarred and torn by battle though the Jotun ships were, of the Aesir vessels I saw nothing but floating wreckage.

"Skoal to Aegir and Niord!" shouted Thor. "Skoal to the sea-kings who have gone to Viking death beneath the waves!"

A clanging like the din of doom beat from the gates before us as the Jotun horde upon the bridge sought to batter them down. We worked at Thor's orders, hastily piling blocks of stone to hold the sagging gates. Then into our midst a wild-faced Aesir warrior came running. He shouted over the clangor and the terrifying roll of loud thunder.

"Loki's forces come upon us in their ships!" he yelled. "They seek to land in our harbor!"

Thor uttered a fierce cry as he stared down at the stormy sea. The Jotun fleet was moving along the coast, the ships jammed with men, heading for the unprotected fiord in the eastern cliffs of Asgard.

"They try to force entrance to Asgard from the harbor — and we have but few guards there!" Thor roared.

"Vidar, hold these gates! Half of you come with me to hold the harbor!"

The bearded giant ran with mighty strides toward the eastern edge of Asgard island. Half of us followed him. The storm was now buffeting Asgard with full force. Lightning burned in sheets and stabs across the night-black sky. Torchlight was flaring from the dark, mountainous mass of Valhalla, whence came through the tempest the dim wailing of women's voices as Odin's body was borne home.

Out of the storm-seared dusk, a slim, mail-clad figure darted to my side as I hastened with Thor and our scant force of warriors toward the eastern cliff. It was Freya, wearing her mail and helmet, holding a shield and light bow in her hand.

"Jarl Keith!" she cried. "I feared you slain in yon terrible battle! I leave you no more!"

"You can't stay with me!" I protested. "We go to hold the harbor against Loki's new assault."

"Then I fight with you!" she said fiercely. "If doom comes now upon Asgard, I meet it at your side."

I could not turn her from her relentless purpose. She ran lightly beside me as we hastened after Thor down the first steps of the narrow cliffside stair. Lightning washed the cliffs, and the deafening crack of thunder drowned the shrieking winds and boom of the sea. By the flashing flares, we saw the Jotun ships already sweeping quickly into the narrow fiord below us. Behind them in the raging sea swam something long, black and sinuous, a great, incredible shape.

"Iormungandr comes with his master Loki!" boomed Thor. "It is well!"

Before we were down the stair, the Jotuns were landing below. Overwhelming the small force of Aesir guards there, they rushed up to meet us.

I swung Freya behind me.

"Keep at my back," I ordered.

"I am not afraid!" argued her clear voice in my ear. Her bow twanged, and an arrow sped down into the throat of the foremost of the swarming Jotuns. I saw Loki leaping ashore from one of the ships. Then the nearest Jotuns reached us.

CHAPTER XX

Ragnarok

THOR'S HAMMER smashed down, and the first two Jotuns fell back with crushed skulls. They pitched off the stair to the depths below. Arrows from enemy archers farther down the stair whizzed up through the lightning-seared dusk and rattled off our mail, or struck down men among us. Freya's bow kept twanging. Each time she loosed an arrow, her clear cry sang loud in my ears.

I tried to keep her near me as I fought beside Thor and tall Vali, desperately trying to hold back the Jotuns. But the stair was wide enough only for three of us to fight abreast. Thor, crimson with blood from many wounds, swung his hammer like a demon of destruction. Yet we were forced up the stairs. Vali dropped with an arrow in his eye, and an Aesir from behind rushed to take his place.

Upward we were pushed, to the top of the stair, the very edge of the cliff. There we hacked with sword and ax. The terrible weapon of the Hammerer whirled and screamed with such fury that the Jotuns could not force the narrow way.

"Make way for me!" pealed Loki's silver voice from below, through the clash of battle and the storm's roar. "I will force the way!"

"I am waiting for you, Loki!" bellowed Thor to the arch-traitor.

Lightning flared again in a continuous blinding flame. It showed Loki's golden helmet flashing up amid the Jotuns crowded on the stair. And it showed, too, a slimy, black, scaly monster whose coils rippled up the steps as it advanced before its master.

"Iormungandr comes!" cried Freya. "The Midgard serpent!"

The Jotuns hugged the cliff side of the stair. Even they were appalled by their dread ally as the incredible snake writhed up toward us. Thor raised his hammer high. Like a shooting black thunderbolt, Iormungandr propelled himself at the bearded giant.

In the lightning streak, I saw the snake's giant spade-shaped head darting with the speed of light. Its opaline eyes were coldly blazing. Its opened jaws emitted a flood of fine, green poison-spray that covered Thor's crimsoned figure.

"My oath to Frey!" roared Thor, and his hammer flashed down.

The snake, with more than human speed, swerved to avoid that terrific blow. But not so swift as Thor's stroke was its swerve. The steel head of Miolnir smashed down upon the spade-shaped head and ground it into the rock of the stair. The hammer itself shivered to fragments from that tremendous stroke.

Iormungandr's monstrous body writhed in its death-throes, flinging Jotuns from the stair to death. Then the serpent's great body fell over the edge, dropping to the sea far below.

"Slain — my wolf and serpent slain!" raged Loki's voice. "Vengeance, Jotuns! Vengeance on Thor!"

The giant was staggering almost helplessly. The helve of his broken hammer suddenly fell from his hand. His red face grew pallid through the blood and green poison that coated it. I sprang with Freya to support him. The few score Aesir warriors left were trying to hold back the Jotuns. Loki's sword was stabbing in deadly strokes among them.

"I am sped," gasped Thor. "The poison of Iormungandr enters my wounds. Help me to Valhalla, for Asgard is lost. There still remains that which Odin bade me do."

Freya and I stumbled with the reeling giant away from that hopeless battle. Our last Aesir warriors could not hope to hold back Loki and his ravening horde. The unending drum-roll of thunder was crashing over Asgard. By the sheeted lightning, we saw Aesir women running calmly to stand beside their men in death. We staggered with Thor into the torchlit entrance of Valhalla castle.

"To the chamber of — the pit-road — to deep Muspelheim — take me there!" Thor gasped.

As we entered Valhalla castle, I heard a wild, wolflike shout of triumph behind us. I looked back. The last Aesir resistance had been overcome, and Loki and the Jotuns were pouring onto the lofty plateau of Asgard. Some of the Jotuns already were running to open Asgard gates to those who battered them from Bifrost Bridge. Women who had rushed out to seek their dead mates were being cut down everywhere.

"Asgard has fallen!" moaned Freya, her blue eyes stricken in the lightning flare. "Loki triumphs!"

"No!" cried Thor in a startlingly great voice. "Never shall Loki reign triumphant in these halls. Lead me on!"

Freya snatched a torch from a socket as we entered the passages of Valhalla. We stumbled past the great hall where Frigga still sat motionless beside Odin's body. On we went, down into the dark passages to the chamber of the pit that led to fiery Muspelheim.

Swaying blindly, Thor pressed the runes on the door with a swiftly failing hand. The door swung open and we entered. Immediately the bearded giant crumpled standing against a wall. Fighting to retain consciousness, he pointed to the square silver box that held the remote control of the sea-gate in the roof of the fiery underworld.

"Give me that control box, Jarl Keith," he whispered in a weakening voice, "that I may open the gate far below and let the waters of the sea rush down into Muspelheim upon the atomic fires. It was my father Odin's order to me. Yes, the atomic fires will be smothered and their radiations will be ended. This will no longer be a place of eternal youth and warmth."

"But when the sea water strikes Muspelheim, there will be an explosion that will wreck this land!" I protested.

"And that, too, would be well!" Thor shouted, swaying. "Let the land be wrecked before Loki and the Jotuns reap fruit of their victory and become a dread menace to all the rest of Earth. It was Odin's warning — Loki must not be allowed to menace all the world!"

He fell heavily to the floor. But he raised his great head and his voice came chokingly:

"Give me the box!"

I heard the quickly approaching roar of Jotun voices from Valhalla's halls above. I heard the shriek of the last Aesir women being cut down by the followers of Loki. In my mind unfolded a shocking vision of Loki, using his overwhelming powers of evil science to dominate all the outside world. I sprang toward the silver control box and was turning to hand it to dying Thor, when Freya screamed.

A man burst into the chamber. Loki's angelic face was a hell-mask of rage. The sword glittered in his hand and his blue eyes were blazing.

"I knew the Aesir would seek thus with my own ancient handiwork to snatch triumph from me by destruction," he said. "But you are too late."

He sprang at me with tiger swiftness, his sword raised. I ripped out my own weapon, but Loki's blade was already stabbing through my shoulder like a white-hot iron. I reeled, senses failing from that agony, dropping the silver control box. Freya darted forward with a wrathful cry, and I saw Loki hurl her back against the wall.

"You have lost, Aesir!" taunted Loki maliciously. "Asgard is mine, and the last Aesir falls to the swords of my Jotuns."

He did not see the great shape rising behind him. Thor, roused by sound of Loki's hated voice, had clutched the rock wall with his nerveless, bloodily tattered fingers and dragged himself erect. Involuntarily I recoiled from the staggering, ominous, black-fleshed figure. But Loki was caught unprepared. The giant hands stole close — and clutched Loki's white neck!

"Turn the knob upon the control box, Jarl Keith!" Thor roared.

Loki stabbed his dagger blindly and furiously back into Thor's breast, battling venomously to free himself. I lunged forward and snatched up the silver box. I seized the knob upon it and turned it as far as it would go.

From the pit-mouth at the center of the chamber came a dull, distant roar of rushing waters. Then a terrific shock rocked Asgard to its foundations. Blinding steam swirled up from the pit with a ravening sound.

"Fool!" shrieked Loki as he tore free from dying Thor.

He hurled himself at me, seeking to snatch the control box from my grasp. I thrust him back with the last of my strength. Through the scalding steam that filled the chamber, Loki staggered backward — and reeled straight into the pit!

A fading scream came up from the roaring cloud of steam as he plunged down into the abyss . . .

All Valhalla castle was rocking wildly above us. One fearful earth-shock followed another. Wild yells of panic chorused from above, coming thinly through the tumult of grinding mountains. Freya was flung against the stone floor, and I stooped frantically over her.

"It is well!" choked Thor. "Asgard and Midgard shall die with the Aesir!" As he sagged to the floor, he raised his dying face toward me. "Save Freya if you can, Jarl Keith. If you can reach your flying ship, you may escape the death that stoops now over all this land."

His eyes blazed up with the last light of fast departing life. For a moment his voice rolled out as strongly as of old.

"Skoal to the Aesir! Skoal to the great race that is gone forever!"

Then his bearded face sagged to the floor in death.

I helped Freya to her feet and dragged her out of that scalding, steam-filled chamber. The Earth-shocks were becoming more violent with each moment. The crash of falling masonry was ominously loud.

"We can't stay here any longer!" I cried to her. "But if we can get to my plane, we can escape."

"Let me die here with my people," Freya moaned, her white face agonized. Abruptly her eyes cleared and she clasped my arm. "No, Jarl Keith. Even now I wish to live for you. But can we escape?"

I stumbled with her up through the shaking, grinding halls of Valhalla castle. The Jotuns had fled or been buried. The scene outside the castle was appalling. Storm still blackened the sky. Lightning flared and thunder roared, but all noises were drowned by the terrible grinding crash of the Earth-shocks.

The castles around the edge of Asgard were being shaken down into ruined masses of masonry. The Jotuns were fleeing wildly down toward their ships in the fiord.

I hastened with Freya toward Bifrost Bridge. A terrible roar beneath us heralded the new shock that flung us off our feet. From cracks splitting in the solid rock of Asgard, wild clouds of steam rushed up. There was a prolonged roar of falling stone. Freya cried out. I looked back just in time to see great Valhalla collapsing into flaming, tumbling ruin.

By this time we had reached Bifrost Bridge and were stumbling precariously across that corpse-littered, dizzy, trembling span. The rainbow bridge abruptly rocked beneath us, threatening to throw us into the crazily boiling sea far below. Some Jotuns were escaping ahead of us, paying no attention to us in their mad panic.

My plane suddenly loomed out of the stormy dusk. The Jotuns, in their fierce eagerness to get into Asgard, had not even molested it. I pulled Freya into the cabin. The rocket motor roared into life, and the plane rushed along the quaking field and lurched into the air. Upward we climbed, the ship bucking and rocking in the terrific currents.

As we climbed higher and headed northward, I saw the full extent of the disaster that had smitten the hidden land. Midgard and Asgard, rocking wildly and shaking the rainbow bridge between them into fragments, were sinking into the sea, shrouded with steam.

The titanic explosion caused by the inrush of sea upon the raging atomic fires of Muspelheim was forcing the whole land to collapse upon that buried underworld. Before our eyes, as I fought to keep the plane aloft, the land solemnly sank.

There was nothing but sea and veils of steam. The blind-spot refraction around the whole land instantly vanished. The rhyme of the rune key had been fulfilled.

Ragnarok had come — the twilight and doom of the Aesir, destroying them and their amazing, wonderful civilization — and also their destroyer . . .

EPILOGUE

OF MY great adventure, little remains to tell. Our night back across the frozen ocean to the expedition's schooner was without mishap. I shall never forget the amazement of Doctor Carrul and the rest of the expedition's members, when I landed my rocket plane beside the *Peter Saul*. Feverishly they asked excited questions when they saw Freya and the bloodstained, battered helmets and mail we wore.

I told them the truth, though I suppose I should have known they could not believe my story. But for their disbelief, I cared little. Nor did I care about what happened after our return to New York. The expedition included in its report a statement that Keith Masters, physicist and pilot, had returned in a delirious condition. They said I had been caught in an Arctic storm, and had brought with me a woman who was obviously a survivor from some storm-wrecked Norwegian ship.

I know now that the smug skepticism of modern men is not to be shaken lightly. Far in the north, beneath the frozen ocean, lie the shattered ruins of the hidden land I trod. Though men may some day penetrate to that submerged, lost land and lay bare the broken stones that once were Asgard's proud castles, they will not wholly believe.

Nor can I entirely blame them. For there are times when even to me all that I experienced takes on the semblance of a dream. It certainly seems like a dream that I rode over Bifrost Bridge with Odin and the warriors of Asgard. Did I really sit in Valhalla's high hall and feast with the nobles and captains of the Aesir? How can I be sure I fought side by side with Thor against Loki and his hordes, on that last great day?

But to reassure myself that it was no dream, I have only to turn and smile gratefully at Freya, my wife. She is dressed now in modern garb, but with the same bright golden hair, sea-blue eyes and slender grace as when I met her first on the cliffs of Midgard. For always Freya is beside me, and not one day have we ever been separated, nor will we ever be.

We do not speak often of lost Asgard and its people, though always they are in my mind as I know they are in hers. But on one night each year, the night of that doomsday eve when we feasted in Valhalla before the coming of the enemy, I pour wine into two glasses and we drink a toast. And our toast is in the words that Thor spoke from dying lips.

"Skoal to the Aesir, to the great race that is gone forever!" I say as I raise my glass.

And from across the table comes Freya's sweet, sorrow-filled voice, whispering her reply.

"Skoal!"

And we drink in memory of the greatest people Earth has ever known.

THE END